I'll Keep You Close

I'll Ke
Y

This is an Em Querido book
Published by Levine Querido

LQ

LEVINE QUERIDO

www.levinequerido.com • info@levinequerido.com
Levine Querido is distributed by Chronicle Books, LLC
Originally published as *Ik zal je bewaren* by Querido.
Text copyright © 2020 by Jeska Verstegen
Translation copyright © 2021 by Bill Nagelkerke
Library of Congress Control Number: 2021931868
ISBN: 978-1-64614-111-1
Printed and bound in China

Published October 2021
First Printing
This publication has been made possible with financial
support from the Dutch Foundation for Literature.

N ederlands
letterenfonds
dutch foundation
for literature

ep

ou

by JESKA VERSTEGEN

translated by BILL NAGELKERKE

Close

LQ

LEVINE QUERIDO

Montclair | Amsterdam | Hoboken

PART I

Journey

A school is a kind of monster with a belly full of children. In the morning it gobbles children up, and in the afternoon it spits them all out again. Me included.

I walk home, taking care when I cross the road.

Autumn leaves aren't careful; they cross over without looking left or right.

I open my palms wide to try and catch whirling, golden leaves.

"Hey, Jesje!" Lienke, the girl from next door, bikes past, laughing.

"Hey!" I call back quickly before looking down hopefully at my hands. Completely empty.

I balance on the edge of the sidewalk. The wind teases me and I lose my balance. One foot in the sea, help! I quickly pull it back onto the sidewalk.

A tall tree grows in the small square next to our house. It stands guard. Come sun, rain, wind, snow, it is there. Come anger, fear, joy, sadness, it is there. I wave to it. Its windswept crown waves back.

I step onto the red gravel of our driveway. When you walk on it, it sounds like you're crunching on a cookie.

I stand in front of the sliding door at the back of the

house that lets you enter through the garden, and see myself reflected in the glass. An eleven-year-old girl, gray-green eyes, slight build, with a pale face and long dark hair. Slowly, I slide the door open.

Doorbell

I know straightaway that Mama is home because I can hear the curtain of music she's drawn around herself.

She puts Mozart on the CD player whenever she's had enough of the outside world. Sometimes she closes the actual drapes as well, making the daylight disappear. If she could, she would let the world dissolve, like sugar in warm tea.

As soon as I come inside, I put my coat on a chair to the left, under the stairs. With both hands, I close the sliding door.

The dining room, which merges into the living room, is full of things, each with its own story: books everywhere, fossils, antique glass in all different colors, a small silver mirror, a little traveling alarm clock that never travels anywhere, pictures, paintings, and a music box.

The music box belongs to Bomma. We haven't had it very long. When Bomma wasn't able to stay in her own apartment in Antwerp any longer, she moved to the nursing home in our town. She had to get rid of nearly all her things, even her own bed, but she held on to the Flemish name for grandmother: Bomma.

"Hello," I call out.

"I'm on the landing," Mama calls back.

• • •

I slip between two of the staircase railings and head up to the landing.

My mother sits on a stool, tucked behind a giant potted golden cane palm. Beside her is the sewing basket and on her lap is one of Papa's shirts. She holds a light blue thread between her thumb and forefinger, deftly passing it through the eye of the needle.

I sit beside her on the floor, watching how she gently holds the fabric and sews a small hem. She can do it so very neatly.

When she's finished, she cuts the thread. "Want to have a try?" she asks.

I nod, taking the needle and fabric from her.

"Easy does it," she warns me.

I drape the shirt awkwardly over my lap.

I smell the scent of laundry detergent and of my father. They're woven into the fabric.

"Bomma taught me." Mama snips a length of thread from the reel and passes it to me. "Wet the end with saliva— it's easier to get it through the eye that way."

I try. When it doesn't work, I lose patience. But I keep trying, and after a few more attempts, I manage it and begin stitching. My hem doesn't look very neat at all.

The doorbell rings. Good timing.

I glance at my mother and see her frightened look.

She stares into the distance before making an uncertain attempt to get up.

"I'll answer it," I say quickly.

"Thanks, love, that would be a great help."

I race down.

"Be careful on the stairs!" she calls out after me.

The bobbled glass of the front door disguises anyone behind it.

Who is it this time? Father Christmas? I smile to myself.

"Good afternoon," a woman says. "I'm collecting for the Red Cross."

I turn to the little old table by the front door. There's a bunch of dried honesty flowers on top; their almost see-through seed pods look like coins. We call it the Tally Table. Papa says that, long ago, money was exchanged on it and coins were tested to see if they were genuine or not. Now it just holds some ordinary small change in its drawer.

I give the lady a guilder. "Bye."

"A collector," I say when I return.

"Hmm," says Mama, absently. She's unpicked my thread and, with her perfect stitches, finishes the hem.

She gets my summer jacket. "You need a new one." She shows me the torn lining. "There's no point mending it again. Your arms stick out of the sleeves. Now that autumn's arrived, the summer jackets are all on sale. We'll go into the city soon."

"Do we have to?" I ask, thinking about all the happy memories attached to that jacket. Playing outside in the sun, building huts, collecting seeds from the balsam plants. The lovely way the balsam pods pop open in your hand.

"Yes," says Mama. "This one's had it. You've outgrown it."

Goodbye jacket, I think. I didn't want to outgrow you. Really, I didn't. I didn't notice; it just happened, and my skin had to go along with it, whether it wanted to or not.

Island

"Tea with gingerbread?" my mother asks.

I leap down the stairs.

"Careful," she says.

I come to a standstill on the last step and slip between the railings again. Mama doesn't know why I do this. No one knows, except me. I do it to check that I'm not growing too fast. As long as I can still fit through, everything's fine.

My mother fills the kettle.

From my pants pocket I take a straight twig sharpened to a point. "Look."

She takes the wood from me. "Very nice," she says, and hands it back.

"I sharpened it on the paving stones at school. I colored the tip black, and now it's a trick pencil."

Mama nods. "I don't care much for tricking people."

The kettle begins to whistle gently.

"*Cry, baby, cry,*" Mama murmurs, taking it off the gas before it howls.

I lay the pencil on the table and help put out the teacups.

My sister, five years older than me, whirls inside. "Pen," she cries. "I need a pen!"

Meanwhile, she's muttering an address over and over to herself.

She grabs my pencil, tries writing with it, huffs with annoyance, and throws it aside. I quickly stuff it into my pocket. Playing tricks is fun.

My sister snatches a slice of cake and goes upstairs to her room, still repeating the address.

I'm sipping some warm tea when someone knocks on the sliding door. It's Lienke behind the glass.

I spring up and open the door.

"Coming to play?" she asks.

I turn to Mama.

"Okay, but only till half past five. And finish your gingerbread first. Lienke, do you want some?"

"Yes, please."

Lienke always speaks politely, eats nicely, and sits as straight as a ramrod. Even the freckles dotted around her nose are arranged in an orderly way.

Lienke picks up the cup the only way she can. Her hands don't open fully. Her fingers are curved, like ten question marks. Once in a while, I see them when we're playing; the big scar tissue on her palms.

"What should we do?" I ask as soon as we're outside. "Make leaf collages?"

Lienke makes a face. Her freckles squish up close together. "Should we go to my place and make something there?"

"Fine, making stuff is always fun."

"Hello," Lienke's mother greets us. "Coming inside to play? How lovely."

The furniture in Lienke's house is light, while ours is dark. Everything here seems lighter than at our place.

Their house is the same size and shape as ours, yet it's completely different inside.

We go and sit at a big white table on the landing.

"What should we make?" I ask.

"My oma's coming to visit soon," says Lienke. "Do you know where she was born?"

I shake my head.

"In Indonesia!"

Lienke gets up and runs to her room. She's soon back with a fat atlas, which she throws open. Her hands slide over the pages like small hills.

Her serious face makes her look older. Luckily, she's got those freckles.

"Here it is!" she cries happily.

"Cel-le-bes," I slowly read.

"No! CE-LE-bes," she says. "That's how it's pronounced. It's an island."

"Oh, right, should we make an island then?" I say quickly. I'd rather talk about anything other than geography.

Lienke's all for it. "Yes, that's a good idea. We'll need a big piece of cardboard!"

Lienke gets some cardboard and art supplies from downstairs, and I smell their aroma. I can already see an island taking shape.

"It has to have a funny outline," I think out loud.

"Like a fried egg," Lienke replies.

I choose a pencil and push the point over the uneven surface of the cardboard.

"I want a bay!" Lienke says.

"Of course," I say.

The lines meet, and the outline is done.

"Could you cut it out?" Lienke asks.

Cutting it out is hard, but after a while an island lies in front of us.

"Should we paint it?"

"Yes, green all over!" I say.

Lienke hands me the paint and I unscrew the lid.

"*Green as grass, green as grass,*" I sing to myself as I spread out big blobs of paint.

The poster paint dries quickly.

"An island needs a mountain," says Lienke.

"Got any clay?" I ask.

Lienke fetches a small packet. She tries to open it but can't manage.

I reach out for it.

Together we shape the mountain.

It has dents all over it, pressed in by our fingers.

"It's already looking great," I say. "But it needs a name."

"Yes," Lienke agrees.

Suddenly, I'm on the alert: "What's the time?"

Lienke checks her watch. "Nearly half past five."

"I've got to get home," I say, flustered.

I hate time. I've only ever once worn the watch I got for my birthday. My wrist looked so grown-up that day that I decided never to wear a watch again.

It's already getting dark as I run home. Don't be late, don't be late! If I'm not on time, my mother's face corrugates with anger.

And when she's angry . . .

As soon as I step into the garden, a black cat bounds away.

I open the sliding door. My glance falls on the travel clock in the cabinet: just in time.

Moz

Outside, the air smells fresh. I hear rustling; the garden's alive.

I spy a movement in the bushes, so I sit back on my haunches.

It's an animal. I'm not scared of it, even when it approaches me.

"Hi there," I say gently to an enormous black cat.

I'm sure it's a male. He's nearly as big as a panther!

Warily, the cat sniffs at my outstretched hand. His light-green eyes investigate me.

"Are you just passing through?" I whisper.

His whiskers tickle my hand.

He sits, his tail curling around his body.

I sit cross-legged beside him.

The cat makes a soft purring sound.

We're a bit alike, I think. We both have dark hair, light eyes, and neither of us is moving.

"What's your name?" I ask.

The cat looks straight ahead.

Music ripples quietly from the house.

Mama has put Mozart on.

"I'll call you Moz," I whisper.

Moz looks satisfied. At least, that's what I think.

We survey the garden, he as a cat, me as a kid.

Music Box

In my imagination, I'm wandering down the zigzaggy paths of the island Lienke and I have created. Where should the waterfall go? And the palm trees? I daydream everything so vividly that I can feel sand tickling between my toes, hear seagulls mewing, and smell the sea.

My visit to the island lasts only a few seconds. Suddenly, I'm back to ordinary life in my bedroom: the yellow bean-bag, my bed, my stuffed toys, and, in the little cubbies in the cabinet against the wall, my treasures. Beside a fragile glass bird is a small doll.

"Hello, Bessie Blue," I whisper. I bought her with my pocket money during the summer holidays. I feel happy whenever I see her. I'm already eleven, probably too old for a doll, but it's so nice to have a small friend who's always close by. I put her in my pants pocket.

Papa sits at the table, hidden behind his newspaper. Mama drinks tea and my sister comes sleepy-eyed down the stairs.

Weekdays always seem the same.

"By the way, Ma," says my sister, as if she's only just waking up properly now. "I want an Arafat scarf."

Mama looks questioningly at her. "From the PLO . . . ?"

Papa lowers the newspaper. "Arafat. Yes, a simmering war, a conflict between two countries, between Israel and . . ."

My mother takes another sip of tea, then sets her cup down harder than she needs to.

No war talk at the table, I guess.

"No, no," says my sister. "It's got nothing to do with politics. I just mean one of those hippie, black-and-white checkered scarves. You're not with it if you don't have one."

Mama stands up. "You'll get your pocket money soon."

I look at the music box in the bookcase. Its lovely *pling-plong* sound used to be heard in Bomma and Bompa's apartment. All of a sudden, I'm transported. I smell the scent of coffee and homemade shortbread again; a candleholder with copper-colored horses sparkles on the mantelpiece; the horses dance in the candlelight.

Bompa snaffled not one but two pieces of shortbread, while Bomma read so animatedly from English storybooks that I understood everything she said. In the Belgian streets, the Antwerp dialect sounded both strange and familiar to me. It was not quite the same Dutch I was used to speaking with my family. Ordinary words, when spoken in the Antwerp dialect, got a new meaning: *clapping* became *chatting* and *punishment* became *unbelievable*.

I turn the little handle of the music box. The first faint sounds trickle out.

It's like a dream.

When Bompa died, those days died with him. Bomma came here, to the Netherlands, to live closer to us.

My mother's voice brings me back to Earth. "Time to go to school."

Reluctantly, I pick up my coat.

"Stand straight, shoulders back."

I quickly straighten up.

As I head outside, I can still hear the *plings* and *plongs*.

In the schoolyard, kids huddle in groups.

Veerle, who's in my class, is standing beneath the tall tree. She's biting the side of her index finger. She often does that during class as well. She chews her fingers as if they're carrots.

When she sees me, she waves with the hand she was just nibbling on.

I head toward her. "Hey."

"Hey," says Veerle. Her gaze wanders over the schoolyard again, and now she pushes her little finger against her front teeth.

There's a nice straight twig on the ground. Perfect for a second trick pencil!

I sit on the ground, carefully sharpening the wood on the paving stones. Slowly, a point takes shape.

I glance up. I don't know why.

Veerle, still gnawing, stares wide-eyed at the school entrance.

Has something happened?

Irene's there at the entrance. Some of the kids point at her. Some pretend not to notice, but they're gawking anyway.

Irene looks down at her feet.

Is she crying?

I watch her run to the school door and ring the bell.

Then I see why: Her skin is tinged a pale blue! It looks quite strange.

"She's turned into a Smurf!" Michiel yells across the schoolyard. He laughs at his own joke.

I push the almost-pencil into my coat pocket.

Mr. Schouderland pokes his head outside. Concerned, he puts his hand on Irene's shoulder. Together, they go inside.

Lienke comes over to me. "Hi," she says. "What's up with Irene?"

I shake my head. "I don't know."

All the commotion makes Veerle gnaw even harder, this time on her thumb.

"Erik says she's got some sort of sickness," says Lienke.

"Are you sure?" I ask. "What is it she has, then?"

"She looks blue. Her hands, arms, head, everything."

"That means you're sick," says Veerle. "It absolutely does. And contagious. Really contagious."

I think of my mother. She works in a nursing home. She's never mentioned blue people. But she doesn't talk much about her work. "As soon as I shut the door behind me, I forget all about it," she often says. Perhaps I should call her? She's bound to know what needs to be done for Irene. She always has an answer for everything.

A little while later, Irene's mother arrives. Irene races out of school and clutches her mother's hand with both of hers. Together, they leave the schoolyard.

History Lesson

Veerle checks her own hands. They aren't blue, but they're red from all the chewing.

Just as I start to inspect mine, the school bell rings.

I head slowly to the entrance.

"She'd better stay out of my way when she comes back," I hear Michiel say. "I don't want to catch it!"

The buzz of the students sounds different today.

I go and sit at my desk: a good spot, halfway down the classroom.

Kids clatter in. Michiel is still wearing his coat when he takes his seat.

Mr. Schouderland doesn't stand for any nonsense. "Michiel, take your coat off and hang it up."

Sulking, Michiel leaves the classroom.

Suzanne giggles when Maartje pokes a black tongue out at her. "I haven't caught it! I've eaten heaps of licorice."

At last everyone is sitting down. Except Irene, of course, since she's gone home.

Is she really ill? What happens when you turn blue? What color comes next? Perhaps all the colors of the rainbow, and after that you're cured. Or will things happen the way they do in that book by Roald Dahl, where a girl turns blue and then changes into a blueberry?

Veerle taps my arm. She whispers: "It's fatal. I've just heard."

In my imagination, Irene turns black and, after that, deathly pale.

I don't say anything. I stick my hands in my sweater. I turn to Irene's empty chair, next to Jasper's. Looking as white as a sheet, he's sitting on the edge of his seat, as if he's about to leap off it any second.

"Let's get started," says Mr. Schouderland.

Mr. Schouderland is going bald. His hairline is shaped like a small harbor where two boats could anchor. His glasses make his blue eyes look bigger than they really are. Deep lines pull down the corners of his mouth, making him look permanently worried.

"History books on desks," he says. "Page forty-six."

I get my book. I'm amazed he hasn't said anything about Irene. That must mean we're not allowed to know. Is it a kind of secret because it's so contagious?

After flicking through the pages, I read on page forty-six: *The Second World War.*

"In our next unit we'll be learning about a war," says Mr. Schouderland as his eyes survey the whole class. "The Second World War."

Michiel puts his hand up, speaking out of turn. "Lots of bombs and dead people, right?"

"Dead people . . ." Veerle repeats, agitated. Her cheeks are red.

Mr. Schouderland puts his finger to his lips. You'd hardly notice him shake his head. But it's just enough because Michiel's hand, shoulders, and mouth all sink. "Consider this," says Mr. Schouderland. "Could ordinary life carry on during a war?"

In my mind's eye, I see people in khaki, bombs everywhere, and . . . and I don't know what.

Imagining something like a carnival, for instance, is easy. War isn't.

I see Jasper staring at Irene's empty chair. Where is she now?

Veerle is chewing again, while Lienke pays close attention to Mr. Schouderland. I'd better do the same.

"Perhaps you're thinking it was all guns blazing, like in some movies," says Mr. Schouderland. "But at the start of the Second World War, life went on as before. It didn't change straightaway, except for the fact that there were a lot of German soldiers in the streets. People went to work, they ate, and they slept. Or they worried about exams, because schools also carried on as usual."

Mr. Schouderland points to a photo in the history book. "This is a photo of Hitler. He was Germany's leader. He had grand plans and wanted to occupy Europe. Ideally, he wanted to conquer the whole world. So the Germans invaded other countries." He stands up, hands on his hips. "Who's been to Rotterdam?"

Some kids raise their hands. I should raise my hand too. But I don't.

Mr. Schouderland looks around the class. "German bombers turned that city into an inferno. A great deal of it was destroyed. The Dutch government was so shaken by the attack, it decided to surrender. That was in May 1940, and after that the Netherlands was occupied by Germany."

That's a familiar year, I think. It's the year my father was born! My mother was born earlier, in 1938.

"War destroys so much," says Mr. Schouderland, "and this was just the beginning of the Second World War." He glances at Jasper. "Who can tell me what sort of planes were flown back then?"

Michiel and a few other boys raise their hands.

My thoughts drift away.

Mama and Papa must have lived through the war. They talk about the past now and again, but never about the war.

Papa works for the newspaper. Sometimes he mentions the war between Iran and Iraq. It's obvious that Mama doesn't like that: She glares and changes the subject.

In a children's magazine, I've read about the nuclear bomb and about the tensions in Israel.

But it's hard to imagine a war.

And certainly not in our town, because nothing much ever happens here.

Hang on, though . . . that's not true.

A man with one leg lives on our street. And farther down, there's a woman who never gets out of bed. And the man in the house on the corner jogs from morning till night. He's as thin as a plank, so perhaps he'll never stop.

I look back at my history book. In one photo, soldiers are marching down a street.

Did they march here as well, past our school, through Gaobert Street? Past Winterman's factory, to the center of town?

Papa said that the Romans once lived here. Perhaps they fought against . . .

"Are you still with us?" Mr. Schouderland frowns at me.

I'm startled. The Romans and all my other daydreams instantly disappear.

Bag

"There you are," my mother says when I arrive home for lunch.

She's just gotten home too. Her handbag is still on the table.

It's an amazing handbag—a Wonder Bag. It's as well-stocked as any warehouse, packed with all kinds of things: paperclips, licorice, foreign money, needle and thread, medicines, and much more. My mother always holds her bag tightly under her left arm.

"School okay?" Mama asks.

"Fine," I say. "Irene turned blue. She had to go home and she's going to die."

Mama looks horrified. "What did you say?"

"She turned blue and she's going to die," I repeat carefully.

"How is that even possible?" Mama shakes her head as if I'm making it all up. "You shouldn't say such silly things."

Maybe I *did* misunderstand what happened. Suddenly, I feel a little ashamed.

"Would you get the knives and forks?" Mama asks. "And remember, this afternoon we're going to the department store to buy a summer jacket on sale. Come straight home."

"Okay," I say absently.

We eat for a while in silence.

"In history, we're learning about the Second World War."

The temperature in the room seems to drop.

Carefully, I look away, since Mama can sometimes get really angry and upset. I don't usually know exactly why. Is that what's going to happen now?

My mother's brow furrows, and her mouth becomes a straight line. She looks fixedly at her plate, cuts her sandwich into small pieces, and lines them up neatly in a row.

Now it's even quieter than it was before.

I imagine the bits of sandwich marching off the plate in an orderly formation.

Mr. Schouderland claps to get our attention. I feel my heart jump, and I bite on my lip.

He scans the class. As soon as he has everyone's attention, he says: "This morning Irene appeared to be ill."

I look at the faces of the other kids. Some frown, others have their eyes wide open in anticipation, and a few look as if they don't want to hear what's coming.

"She's been to see her family doctor . . ." Mr. Schouderland says.

"Is she going to die?" Michiel calls out.

"There's nothing the matter with her." Mr. Schouderland smiles. "The color in Irene's new quilt ran, that's all. That's why her skin looked blue. She'll be back at school tomorrow. She's staying home this afternoon. It gave her a big fright."

I breathe a sigh of relief and look again at the empty chair beside Jasper.

This morning, all of a sudden, Irene wasn't the usual Irene anymore. And everyone behaved differently. Me included. We treated Irene as if she'd become dirty. Blue and dirty.

Time to forget all that. I only want to think about nice things. About the new trick pencil in my pants pocket. It's almost ready! And about Bessie Blue. My little friend, so small she fits in my pants pocket. She'll never leave me in the lurch.

Jacket

Mama is a dietician in a nursing home. She normally works half days, but now and then she works a whole day. Sometimes they call her at home if they need more advice about a patient. Mama puts the phone down. "Right, we can go now," she says.

I stand beside her. She's so small, I realize. We're nearly the same height now. How strange. At that moment, I'm suddenly sure that I'll end up taller than her. But I don't want big breasts and hips—otherwise I won't be able to do cartwheels anymore.

"It only takes twenty minutes to get to town," Mama says. "We'll have that new jacket in no time."

She backs the car down the driveway.

Mama puts on music while we drive and turns the heat to its highest setting. Classical music and warm air compete for space; this car is far too small for piano music, the stifling heat, Mama, *and* me. I wish I could get out.

I unzip my winter coat.

"Irene wasn't sick," I say after a while. "She was blue because the color in her new duvet ran."

My mother smiles. "There you are then; never jump to conclusions."

"How do you mean?"

Mama thinks for a moment. "I mean you shouldn't decide on something before you know all the facts and how to interpret them."

"I was only repeating what Veerle said," I say quietly, feeling even more hot and uncomfortable than before. "I didn't really believe it."

"You should always think for yourself."

I remember feeling relieved when Mr. Schouderland told us it hadn't been anything serious. So I guess I must have believed she was sick.

"What should you do if you don't know all the facts?" I ask.

"Just be honest and say you don't know. Sometimes that's enough. Or you could get more information."

"How?" I ask.

"Well, for instance, you could ask Papa or me," says Mama. "Or go to the library. Books can teach you a lot."

"We're here," says Mama. She parks the car, and I jump out into the fresh air.

Together Mama and I walk to the department store.

She pushes against the revolving door and then heads for the escalator. I hurry after her.

It isn't busy inside. Be careful to step on to the escalator at exactly the right moment. . . . and . . . now! I think I'll hate escalators for as long as I live.

"This is the right place," says Mama. She points to a rack of sale-price summer jackets. "Which one do you like?"

"This one," I say. A jacket with a cheerful checkered pattern. I have it on in an instant.

Mama freezes. "Take it off," she hisses. Her eyes narrow, and her face pales.

Frightened, I take the jacket off.

"No checks," she says. "Put the jacket back."

Her reaction scares me. I want to say something, but nothing seems good enough.

I'd rather go home right now. Jacketless.

"What about this one?" my mother asks. She holds up a boring blue jacket. "Try it on."

Reluctantly I push my arms into the sleeves. It's a vile thing.

"A little roomy," Mama says. "Next year it'll fit you perfectly. Decision made."

I gape at her.

She takes the jacket and walks decisively over to the cashier.

Waiting in line, she says, "We'll be home before dark."

I turn around. A sleeve of the checkered jacket waves goodbye to me from the rack.

Moz

I look through the sliding glass door into the front garden. Something black stalks behind the shrubbery.

Moz!

Abruptly, he bounds across the lawn: There's another cat in the garden.

Moz yowls. He arches his back, fur bristling, before lashing out at the second cat.

It cowers, then sprints away.

Moz! I think, amazed.

I slowly slide open the door and go outside.

"Moz," I call softly.

He becomes curious when he hears my voice, and pads toward me.

I kneel down.

Moz curls himself around me. He butts me with his head, sits beside me, and purrs.

Tentatively, I stroke him. "Have you already forgotten how angry you were just then?"

Moz stretches out his paws; their pads are so gentle and silent when they touch the ground. But his claws tear at the grass.

He might feel soft, but you can't ignore those sharp claws.

Maybe I've got claws as well. Sharp claws that I can

unsheathe . . . like the ones my mother has. Hidden, but there all the same. Ready to use. . . .

But what would I use them for? And would I unsheathe them as unexpectedly as Moz just did?

I stroke his black fur. "It's like I've known you for a long time already," I whisper.

The cat looks at me, headbutts me again, and disappears into the dusk.

Secrets

"Irene?" I ask, before the bell goes. I put my hand on her arm.

She turns around, gives me a quick glance, then looks away again.

I risk a question: "Is everything okay?"

She focuses on the toes of her shoes.

She seems the same as always. The blue tinge is gone from her skin.

But she isn't herself. She always laughs. Not now.

From my pocket, I take the trick-pencil I finished yesterday. "For you," I say.

Irene takes it. "Thanks."

The other kids ignore her.

"Do you want to come and join us by the big tree?"

She shrugs. I hesitate, then walk away by myself.

Veerle's already waiting by the tree. She's impatient. "What were you doing?"

"Just the usual," I say. "Just talking."

She's grumpy. Even her fine hair seems impatient, its loose strands flickering in the wind.

Here's Lienke, right on time.

Then the bell rings. The school takes a bite and swallows us whole.

• • •

Mr. Schouderland straightens his glasses. "Silence please! We'll start the day with language skills."

The lively chatter fades away.

Everything's back to normal, I think.

Lienke places her pencil case neatly in front of her. A little farther away, just as usual, sits Irene. She lifts her head, sees me, and grins.

I grin back.

Yes, today everything's back to normal.

Yesterday's upset was an exception to the rule.

Michiel raises his hand. "Sir, what exactly does it mean to be Jewish?"

Mr. Schouderland doesn't answer right away. He readjusts his glasses. "Why do you ask?"

"Well," says Michiel, "because yesterday we were learning about the Second World War, and Jews and the Second World War go together. That's right, isn't it?"

Mr. Schouderland takes his time to reply. "Being Jewish means belonging to a particular community of people. Judaism has certain religious practices and traditions, just as Catholicism and Islam have. Between 1940 and 1945 there were a great many Jewish victims, murdered by the Germans."

Michiel nods. "But . . ."

Mr. Schouderland gives him a stern look. "The Jews suffered appalling treatment during the war. But we'll come to that in history class. Now it's time for language skills."

Michiel's lips form a new question.

Mr. Schoulderland puts his hands on his hips. Michiel loses his nerve and grudgingly picks up his language book.

"Time for some grammar. Read the first sample sentence in your book. Find the subject of that sentence by asking yourself the appropriate questions."

I lose myself in my thoughts. I think about Michiel's question and Mr. Schouderland's reply.

Jews, victims, dead people.

Death is a part of war. I know that, even if we never talk about the Second World War at home.

I remember the time my father exclaimed during a meal: "Remember the flood of 1953 in Zeeland, which killed so many people! It's a scar on Dutch history."

The Second World War is a scar as well. I think of the word Mr. Schouderland used: *appalling.*

Scars are drawings that tell a horrible story from the past.

How did Lienke get the scars? She's never told me.

I shiver. I take Bessie Blue from my pants pocket. *No playing in class,* Mr. Schouderland often says. But I do, in secret.

School's finally over. I race home. The wind blows so hard at my back, I feel as if I'm flying.

Once I'm home, I sit down to draw at the long antique table in the living room. My parents call it the Chopping Block. The old wood has deep grooves in it, making it impossible to draw a straight line on my paper unless I place something underneath. Even then, the point of my pencil sometimes goes right through the paper. But that doesn't stop me. My picture becomes cheerful and multicolored. I use as many colors as I can.

Bomma

Mama reaches into the glove compartment. "Licorice?"

"Thanks."

We're on our way to see Bomma, who isn't feeling too good.

I suck on the licorice. By the time we drive into the parking lot, it's finished.

The nursing home smells of food and detergent.

All the doors look alike. Only the names beside them differ from one another.

Bomma is proud of her last name, especially her maiden name. It's a name that starts with a Q. Querido. Bomma corrects anyone who doesn't pronounce it properly. "No," she says in irritation. "It's keh-REE-doe, not KWEH-ree-doe."

Mama opens the door.

We go inside without taking off our coats. It's very dark. The drapes in the small room, where the bed is as well, are closed.

"Mother?" Mama asks in a quiet voice.

There's no reply.

I turn to Bomma's bed.

Bomma's eyes are open. Her bony fingers clutch the

sheets. She used to have a grip of iron—she could twist open the lid of any jam jar.

"Hello, dear," Mama says to Bomma.

There's still no reply.

"How is everything?"

I hang back by the foot of the bed.

Mama opens the drapes.

The room brightens. The daylight reveals how things are with Bomma: the box of pills on the table, a dish smeared with some dried-up yogurt, a drinking straw that droops sadly out of a carton of apple juice, Bomma's skin-colored stockings draped over her wheeled walker. It makes me feel very sad.

I look at Bomma and my eyes fill up with tears.

It's as if Bomma is seeing me for the first time. Her mouth drops open and she whispers, "Hesje." She points at me with a thin finger.

Hesje? I think in surprise.

Mama's eyes open wide, shocked by her mother's mistake. "No, mother, this is Jesje," she says gently.

Bomma keeps on staring at me and says with certainty, "Hesje."

"Who's that?" I ask hesitantly.

Mama doesn't answer.

I wonder uneasily if I've done something odd. . . . No, I don't think so. So why is Bomma looking at me like that?

"Do you want to sleep?" Mama asks.

Bomma nods.

Mama tries plumping the pillow. It doesn't want to be plumped.

Bomma's big blue eyes are still fixed on me, as if they're searching for something they've lost.

I want to leave. I push my hands deep into my pockets— luckily, Bessie is there. I wrap my hand around her.

Mama tidies a few more things before closing the drapes.

It's as dark now as it was when we arrived.

Mama gestures toward the door.

"Bye, Bomma," I say quietly. Has she heard me? I take a hand out of my pocket and wave it weakly in her direction. Did she even notice?

A man in a white uniform comes toward us in the hallway.

"Nurse Ferry," says Mama. "Things aren't looking the best . . ."

Ferry enjoys telling Bomma stories while he eats chocolate biscuits, one after another. He laughs at his own jokes and his brown moustache dances on his upper lip.

Bomma loves him.

Ferry and Mama discuss Bomma. Worry lines appear on Mama's face.

Secret

My mother is wearing a pencil skirt, which forces her to take smaller steps than usual.

I reach the car first.

Mama opens the door.

"Who's Hesje?" I ask after the motor starts.

My mother swallows. She takes her time to answer. "Hesje is someone from the past. From long ago."

"So who was she then?"

"She's no longer alive. It doesn't concern you."

I see the muscles in my mother's cheek tighten as she sets her jaw. Asking any more questions would be of no use now. I recognize the signs: She clams up like an oyster, and she won't say another word about it.

Thank goodness it's just a short drive home. The time it takes to finish a single piece of licorice.

Mama starts to prepare dinner. She peels potatoes. She's fast and efficient. Will I ever be able to do it that quickly?

I pick up a knife and try. My potato unpeels into a chunky, angled shape.

Mama doesn't speak. It's quieter than usual. Or am I imagining that?

Not all silences are the same. When I cuddle Moz, I

don't need words; it's a good silence. There are also scary silences—for instance, when Mama thinks I've done something wrong. And then there are angry silences, when people stop talking to each other after an argument.

A sound at last! I hear the crunch of gravel as Papa's car comes up the driveway.

The first thing he does when he gets home is change from his suit into something more relaxing. "Hi, everyone!" he calls out as soon as he comes inside. "I'll just get my comfies on."

There are some words that tell a whole story on their own: *comfies*, for instance.

Fotsekaporre is another. Bomma told me what it means. Fotsekaporre are people's peculiarities. Everybody has them.

What are mine? I never finish all the drink in my cup . . . and I daydream. Too often, maybe. Hesje . . . who on earth is Hesje? Mama's friend at school from long ago? She hardly has any friends now. Practically nobody visits; only family now and then.

"How was it at your mother's?" my father asks once we're at the table.

Mama answers casually, although her face tells a different story. "It went well."

"She thought I was Hesje," I say, watching for Papa's reaction.

Magnified by his glasses, his eyes look big.

My mother gives a tiny shake of her head. She serves the

potatoes, rapping the serving spoon against our plates with more force than usual.

My father notices this too. He scores lines in his potato, the chunky one I peeled.

My sister comes downstairs, carrying a textbook in one hand.

"No books at the table," says my mother.

My sister puts her book aside.

Mama's hiding something. A secret. Something I'm not allowed to know. It's about Hesje. Do my father and sister know about it? Do they know who Hesje was? Maybe it's only me who doesn't? Me, the youngest, always the last to find out.

PART II

Moz

I stand in the garden, breathing in the autumn air.

I think about Hesje. Someone from the past. I don't know her, but, out of the blue, she's now incredibly important to me.

Bomma thought I was Hesje. I must look like her. Or perhaps I sound like Hesje?

But Bomma's ill; she made a mistake. That must be it.

I take Bessie Blue from my pocket. I sit down and make her skip through the grass. I pretend she's on our island, the sun shining on her hat. My sister sometimes thinks I'm childish because I still play with dolls, but I enjoy it.

Meow.

"Moz," I say, thrilled. "There you are."

I stroke the cat.

"Do you have a secret?" I ask.

Moz purrs, and I tickle him.

"If you had one, you'll have forgotten it by now. Cats don't keep secrets in their head."

Prrrr, Moz purrs.

"I wish I was a cat," I whisper.

Moz gracefully stretches out his back paw.

I try to imitate him by sticking my leg up in the air.

Moz looks at me and leaves without saying goodbye.

Sometimes you're with someone, then you're alone again.

Strawberry Jam

I creep across the landing. I'm the first one up this morning!

No, I'm not. I can hear my sister rummaging in her room.

I obey the notice on her door and knock first.

"Yes?"

I open the door.

She glances up, annoyed. "What is it?"

"Nothing important," I murmur. "Well, actually it is."

"Get on with it, then."

"What do you know about Hesje?"

She looks surprised. "I thought she was family. From very long ago. Why?"

I wonder. Mama has a lot of brothers and sisters.

"Hurry up," says my sister with a sigh. "I'm writing an important letter."

I want to ask more, but I feel awkward.

"Can you do something for me?" she asks.

"What?"

"Will you mail this letter? It has to go today. 15 Kromme Molenweg. I can't do it myself."

"Why not?"

"I'll explain later some time. Will you do it?"

"Sure," I reply.

I shut the door. My sister can only focus on her letter.

Hesje was family! Maybe she was one of Mama's sisters?

I look down over the banister. It's still dark in the dining room.

"Morning." Mama comes into view, buttoning up her dressing gown. "Will you help set the table? We're all up early today."

She flicks on the light.

I head to the kitchen.

"Stand straight, shoulders back," my mother says.

Right, I always forget.

Soon we're at the table having breakfast. Even my sister. Her hockey gear waits for her by the sliding door. She butters a sandwich, puts her knees up against the edge of the table, balances her chair on two legs, and takes a bite.

"Don't seesaw," says my mother.

My sister sighs and sinks back into place.

I wonder what to put on my sandwich.

My father spreads strawberry jam onto white bread. "Mmm," he says. "The taste of this takes me back."

"Where to?" I ask.

Papa chews before he answers. "During the war we didn't have a lot to eat, which meant we were always hungry."

Mama frowns, but Papa doesn't notice.

"We got stale bread," he says. "Nothing else. And, in

the evenings, watery cabbage soup. We even ate sugar beet and tulip bulbs. Horrible! But one day, my father came home with strawberry jam. He had to bike a long way to get it—on a bike with wooden wheels that was very hard to pedal. I'll never forget my first mouthful of that strawberry jam."

Mama stands up and begins to clear the table.

I put my coat on before going into the garden.

My sister follows me. Once outside, she rummages around in her sports bag and hands me her letter. "Don't you dare forget it!" she says. "It's a matter of life and death that it gets delivered today."

"But . . ."

"I've got to go—hockey!"

I nod and take the envelope. "I promise."

"Good," she says. She heaves up her hockey gear and hurries off.

I peek at the name on the envelope. It's a letter to some-one named Paul; his name is underlined in red. I recognize the address. It's the one my sister was saying over and over to herself, the one she tried to write down using my fake pencil. I know where the address is. I put the letter close to my chest and zip up my coat.

Tree

The tree in our garden is in exactly the right place. From its branches, I can look over the garden and the street, hidden from sight inside its crown of autumn-colored leaves.

The outdoor table on our patio looks abandoned. It wasn't long ago that we drank lemonade there on warm days. Now it's damp with dew and smothered with leaves.

I think about Papa's strawberry jam story. It happened during the war. The Second World War! Papa and Mama were children then. I try to imagine my parents as six-year-olds. It's so difficult.

I scan the street. There's a ball! A cheerful red color. Forgotten or lost? Should I go and get it?

Hang on, the lady next door is walking by with her dachshund.

She wants me to call her Auntie Meirke even though she's not family. Auntie Meirke's favorite pastime is gossiping. She's very good at it; she knows everything about everyone in the neighborhood.

Her dog wants to play with the ball, but she's not happy about that and pulls on his leash.

Now that she's gone, I can get the ball.

But wait, here comes the paperboy! He's got two bags crammed full of papers slung over the carrier rack at the rear of his bike. He stands on a pedal with one foot while he kicks the ball with his other foot. His bike wobbles before he takes off again. The paperboy bikes around the corner, and the ball rolls in the opposite direction.

That's a shame—now I can't see the ball or the paperboy anymore. He'll be cycling past the garden to our mailbox on Berkakkers Street. I know that for a fact because four different newspapers land on the doormat every day. My father wants to keep on top of the news, four times over. You have to if you're a journalist.

Papa has explained to me the proper way to write a newspaper article. You have to answer a number of important questions about a topic. *Who? What? Where? Why? How? When?* If you can answer all of them, then you know enough to write a complete article.

My mind goes back to Hesje.

I can see Bomma's face in front of me. She thought I was Hesje. Mama and Papa know who she was, but they'd rather keep quiet about it. Their silence only makes me want to learn more. It's like a magnet.

I promise myself I'm going to discover the truth about Hesje. Yes. I'm going find out who she was. *Who? What? Where? How? Why? When?*

I can feel my heart pounding. Is it excitement or fear? I don't know. What will I learn?

I already know a little bit about the *Who.*

How hard can it be to find out the rest of the *Who?* and the *What? Where? How? Why? When?*

I climb down out of the tree. I'm itching to do something right away, but I'm not actually sure what. I look around, walk into the street, and come across the ball I'd spotted earlier. I go and pick it up.

There's no name on it. There's no one around. "Finders keepers," I tell myself. "You're mine now."

I feel the envelope against my chest and remember my promise.

Ball in hand, I skip over to the Kromme Molenweg. My hair bounces along with me.

Why don't adults skip? Do they all of a sudden decide they're too old for it? I hope I never forget how to skip.

Bounce

Ball under my arm, I cross the street.

Is Lienke awake? She sleeps a *lot*.

I head over to her house. Through the glass of the sliding door, I see her mother and father sitting at the table. I knock. Lienke comes running. "I was just coming to see you. Nice ball!"

"Found it!" I say.

"I'll just get my coat," says Lienke.

While I wait, I notice that Lienke's father's shoulders sag a little. He looks pale, his eyes sunken.

Lienke's mother has striking blue eyes that shine below her dark hair. She always looks so proper.

Everything in their house is always spick-and-span. Even their words are carefully arranged in their heads. Mine tumble over themselves to escape my lips. My head's such a messy muddle.

"Are you coming?" Lienke asks. She slides the door closed behind her.

"Yes," I say.

"Want to play curb ball?" she asks, pointing to the ball.

"Good idea," I reply.

"Have you heard the latest?"

"What?"

"They're going to chop down the tree on the square between our houses. My mother heard about it. She works for the council."

My heart misses a beat. I come to a standstill. "Our tree?"

Lienke nods gravely.

"They can't do that!" I say. I carry on walking. "We have to stop it from happening!"

"Agreed," says Lienke.

"Can't your mother do something?" I ask. "After all, she works for the council."

"She says there's nothing more that can be done."

"Then the two of us will have to save the tree!"

"How are we supposed to do that?"

Lienke looks at me conspiratorially.

"When they arrive, we'll go and stand by the tree," I think aloud. "We'll tell the choppers-down that they can't!"

"Yes!" says Lienke, all fired up. "Perhaps we'd better talk about it in code, so no one gets to know our plans. We'll beat them!"

I continue dreaming up ways to save the tree. We'll take the choppers-down by surprise, Lienke and me. Perhaps the two of us will end up in the newspaper: TREE SAVED, written in extra-big letters.

At the same time, I'm still pondering: *Who? What? Where? How? Why? When?*

"Wake up!" Lienke calls. "Bring the ball!"

Oh yeah. I was daydreaming again.

We stand on the curb.

"Here goes!" I throw the ball.

The ball doesn't bounce straight back.

"Missed!" Lienke cries as she catches it.

It's not an easy game. When the ball rebounds from the opposite curb, you have to catch it. If you manage that, then you're allowed to take a step forward. Another good bounce and catch, another step forward, until you reach the other side of the street, and then you've won.

"Pay attention!" Lienke shouts.

She's right, I'm just not with it. I forget to catch the ball, and now it bounces behind me into the bushes. I fish it out and walk back to the curb.

"My father had strawberry jam for breakfast."

Lienke can't help but laugh. "That's earth-shattering news!"

I hold the ball above my head. "He said it reminded him of the Second World War."

Lienke's laughter shuts off, and she says somberly, "My parents talk about it sometimes. How they went hungry and all. They always remind me of it when I'm not hungry or when I leave some food on my plate."

I want to tell Lienke what happened. I want to talk about Hesje and about all the questions that have been dancing around in my head since I found out about her. But something in me—I'm not sure exactly what—holds me back. "No one can be trusted," Mama sometimes says.

I throw the ball.

"Bullseye!"

Gossiping Aunt

Lienke and I head back. I've got the ball clamped under my arm.

"Should we hang out for a while longer?" Lienke asks.

"Great idea!" I say. "We've still got a lot to do on our island."

"Hello, little ladies!" a loud voice hails us. It's our neighbor, Auntie Meirke. Her house is right between the two of ours. "How's everything going?"

"Fine," says Lienke.

I only nod.

"Your grandmother's not very well," says Auntie Meirke, which gives me a jolt.

Auntie Meirke rattles on. "I'm a volunteer at the nursing home, I help out during lunch and coffee time—that's when you get to hear all the news. Oh yes, lots of the old folks who stay in their room all day and don't make it downstairs anymore, well, they go downhill fast. But hear this, young lady, they can claw their way back up again. Yes, I've seen that happen many times as well. I like to sing with the old folk. They enjoy that. Especially the old songs, like 'The Horse and Buggy on the Strand.'

"I tell you what, I've got a brand-new panini press. Would the two of you like to come by for a grilled cheese?

I make them very tasty. My daughter always asks for grilled cheese with ketchup. She's recently left home, just like my eldest."

"I don't know," says Lienke. "I have to eat at home."

"I'll ask your mothers," says Auntie Meirke. "How about we make it next Wednesday for lunch?"

"Um . . ." I begin.

"That's settled then! Bye-bye, little ladies, until next week!"

The short legs of Auntie Meirke's dachshund have trouble keeping up with her.

Lienke giggles. "Oh boy, we've got no choice now."

"Yes," I say. "No choice."

I dwell on what our next-door neighbor said. Are things really going downhill with Bomma? It's no wonder Mama always looks worried. Why didn't she tell me?

Lienke is concerned too. "I didn't know that about your oma."

"Yes, it's horrible," I say.

"Let's go and carry on with our island," Lienke says.

"Yeah, let's. Should we glue on some tiny glass beads for flowers?"

Lienke nods. "I've got some small pebbles—we could use them as well."

We walk to her place in silence, both of us deep in thought.

I always tell Mama everything, even my strange dreams. But she . . .

Oh well, now I've got secrets too. I'm going to find out more about Hesje and save a tree.

"Can you ask your parents when the tree's going to be chopped down?" I ask Lienke urgently. "Can you find out tonight?"

"I can't tonight," says Lienke.

"Tomorrow night, then," I say. "Monday is one flash, Tuesday two, and so on."

A while ago Lienke and I discovered that we could use flashlights to communicate with each other at night. I can see her bedroom from our landing. With a full list of the words we've agreed on, words we've converted into flashes, I stand on the landing in the dark. It's a bit awkward, checking the list quickly and having only a handful of words to build sentences with. Some of the word-flashes we came up with aren't really needed for a flashlight conversation. But there was no way we were going to leave out *dog*, *cat*, and *Smurf snot*.

Deciphering flashes is also tricky. Once, I mistakenly decoded *Dog is rotten*.

"What was that supposed to mean?" I asked Lienke the next day. It actually meant *Mama's coming*.

All the same, flashlight talk is delightfully mysterious.

I was caught once. Mama asked very crossly, "Why are you still up? You should have been in bed ages ago."

So I need to be more careful.

That evening I choose a moss-green notebook. I'm going to record my findings in it. I'll have to try and keep my writing neat, right up to the last page. That's not going to be easy. Every single one of my notebooks, writing pads, or diaries starts off neat but ends up like chicken scratch. My handwriting becomes wilder and wilder, so that near the end it's as if my words are galloping toward the final pages.

Journey of Discovery, I write on the first page, and *Hesje*.

On other pages I put journalistic questions: *Who? What? Where? How? Why? When?* Whenever I make a discovery, I'm going to write it down on the correct page of the notebook. I can already add something under *Who?*: *Hesje is family.*

Photo Album

When we go inside, Bomma is sitting hunched in her chair. The drapes are pushed untidily aside. Her hands rest on an opened book on her lap.

As I give Bomma a kiss I glance curiously at the photo album, but her hands are shielding the old black and white photos, and I can only glimpse the faces from long ago through the gaps between her fingers.

Mama tidies the room: Empty apple juice cartons go into the trash, dirty clothes into the laundry basket. In the midst of all that, she brews coffee.

When Bomma shifts her hands, I see her graceful handwriting beneath the photos. If only I wrote as beautifully as that. I focus on trying to read the words.

"What do you want to drink?" my mother suddenly asks me.

I blush. Did my prying eyes give me away?

"Milk," I say.

Bomma nods her thanks as Mama sets a cup of coffee down in front of her.

Bompa was once the manager of a coffee factory. Coffee is sacred in our family. Liquid gold, they call it. It's a pity that I don't like that sort of gold and neither does my sister.

Bomma carefully closes the book on her lap. She takes a small spoon and slowly stirs her coffee. Her hand trembles.

We drink in silence.

Bomma looks at me, blue eyes in a thin face.

She beckons me over. "Do you want to see it?" she asks, holding up the photo album.

I turn briefly to Mama before quickly reaching out and taking it.

The album stills feels warm, almost as if it's alive. It creaks as I open it.

The first photo is a picture of Bomma when she was young. She's about twenty, I'm guessing, but I recognize her easily. Dark curls frame her face.

"I wanted to be an actress," she tells me. "But that didn't work out, so then I started teaching English."

On the next page there's a man with a beard. He also has dark, wavy hair. He's wearing a black jacket with a high collar. I read the inscription: *Grandfather.*

"My father had two brothers," Bomma murmurs.

They're all memories, I think. Her family, so my family too. I wouldn't be here if it wasn't for them. This feels both strange and familiar.

I turn another page. My great-grandfather's two brothers. The one in the first photo looks like a professor, while the other reminds me of Willy Wonka. Perhaps because of his dark, medium-length hair and the bow tie dancing beneath his chin. Below the first photo, it says *Emanuel Querido*, and below the second, *Israel Querido.*

Bomma's crooked forefinger hovers above the pictures. "They were my father's brothers. This one was a publisher," she says softly. "And this man"—she points to Willy Wonka—"was a famous writer."

The next photo is of a man with a crown of white, curly hair. Small glasses balance on his large nose. He looks a bit cheeky. The woman beside him in the photo must be his wife. I don't think she wanted to be in the photo. Her mouth is turned down in a familiar frown, and her fingertips are pressed together in a fidgety kind of way. I recognize her name! Branca! The same name as my mother's, whose frown is exactly the same.

My mother gets up. Before I have a chance to look at any more of the book, she says, "Okay, we're going now."

I quickly turn one more page. A lady with wavy hair and two children. *My sister, Liesje*, it says in Bomma's elegant handwriting. In an instant I read the other names: *Eddy*, and . . . *Hesje*.

Shut

"A photo album," I say to Mama as we head to the car.

"Yes," she says. "With family photos. Just my family, not Papa's. The photos were taken a long time ago."

"Were any of them at last year's family get-together?"

"No, none of them are around anymore."

I think about the black-and-white photos. So they're not here anymore. Passed away. Dead. Died . . .

"But who . . . ?" I want to ask a new question.

"No," says my mother.

Because of the way she emphasizes the *n*, and her icy tone of voice, I quickly clam up. I know the conversation's done. There's no point asking more questions.

Mama puts her sunglasses on, even though it's cloudy outside, and, in silence, she starts the car.

I bite my lip. When will I be able to take another look at the book?

This will be one of my jobs as a journalist: I have to get to the truth.

It's scary to think that none of the people in the photo album are still around.

The photos are in black and white, making everything seem even longer ago. But my mother knows who they are. Did she ever get to meet them? She sits beside me, in full color, so, really, it can't have been all that long ago.

And my Bomma's still here. Older, of course, but still alive.

Who's still here, and who isn't?

Who is Hesje? I have an uneasy feeling in my stomach.

We drive past the familiar chapel in Dorpsstraat, past the drugstore where large jars of yellow hair gel are on a special sale in the shop window. Home, via the church and the smallest wood I know.

I'm sitting in my beanbag, lost in thought. I close my eyes, remembering Mama's family get-together. My aunts and uncles were there, Bomma and Bompa's six children.

Bomma and Bompa's children have children of their own, my cousins. Those are the only family members who were there that day.

I update my notebook.

My uncles, aunts, and cousins are all still alive. So who are the ones who aren't? Was Liesje from the final photo really Bomma's sister? Did Bomma have any other brothers and sisters? How can I find out?

That evening I stand on the landing in front of the window. I'm an investigative journalist in pajamas. I have a flashlight, a sheet of paper with secret codes, and a pen.

I'm working on my other story: the saving of a tree.

I search the darkness. I see the dark shape of the big old tree on the square. Four houses are grouped around the square. To the left lives Auntie Meirke. To the right is the driveway of another neighbor (who sometimes takes fruit from our apricot tree if she thinks no one is watching). And Lienke's house is just opposite mine. I'm looking right at her bedroom.

The weak light of a street lamp reveals her white-and-red striped drapes. What's keeping her? It must be half past eight already. I'm cold. I wish I'd put on a cardigan. But I can't go now; if I do, she'll show up as soon as I've left.

I flash once with my flashlight. Nothing, no signal from the opposite side.

Impatiently, I smooth the crinkled sheet of paper with the secret ciphers.

I signal again. Still nothing. I'm just about to give up when I spot the flash of a flashlight.

I keep count. One, two, three, four, five, six.

The flashing stops. It's on Saturday, then. That's when the tree's going to be chopped down.

I wait a little longer.

There's nothing further.

I flash her an over-and-out signal: short, long, short, long, short.

I look again at the beautiful tree. It's stands there like a faithful friend. I slink back to my bedroom.

Moz

Meow. Moz meows as if he has something he wants to tell me.

Perhaps how high in the tree he dared to climb. Or how he murdered a mouse. That's a perfectly normal thing for him to do. That's nature. Dead things don't frighten him. They do frighten me though. I used to think that when people died, they deflated, leaving their bodies as flat as a pancake.

My sister arrives home. She's clutching a jar of yellow gel.

One less jar on the drugstore's gel tower. My sister uses gel to help shape her combed-back hair.

"Hi," she says, stroking the cat before heading inside.

I imagine Moz with a gelled tuft of fur. He'd be hip enough then to swing along to the songs on the Top 100 list.

Or would he, like me, rather watch than join in?

Moz slinks toward the bushes.

Slinking is a very useful skill for him. Dogs don't hear you, and it's easy to stalk birds.

Mama wants me to do pretty much the same: *slink.* I'm never allowed to talk too loudly, be too exuberant, be too angry. Everything with *too* in front of it is wrong, especially being too conspicuous.

I'd make a good cat, except for having to kill birds.

Night

I wake up with a start.

My heart races. Did I have a nightmare?

It's dark—still nighttime.

Do I hear voices, or am I imagining them?

I glance at the clock. Half past one. *Half past one?*

Yes, I hear hushed voices.

I quickly push the blankets away. I see a strip of light under my bedroom door. I listen carefully.

Mama and Papa are talking rapidly and tensely to each other downstairs.

"I'll go," says my mother. "The nurse said she was completely confused."

Something's wrong.

My father asks something, though I can't make out what it is.

My mother doesn't answer.

Then the telephone shrills.

Do I dare eavesdrop? Of course I do! I'm a journalist in search of answers, aren't I? I get up, opening the door as noiselessly as I can. I slink across the landing and look down into the dining room. The phone is tucked under the stairs. If I sit on the topmost step and stick only my head between the railings I can just barely see my mother.

I listen.

Mama's voice is strained. "No, dear, you're not on the platform."

On the platform? Who's she talking to?

"You're in your own bed, in the Molenwiek Nursing Home," Mama says softly.

She's talking to Bomma; it can't be anyone else.

"You see people?" Mama asks. "Tell me who they are."

My mother sighs, understanding. The telephone cord taps against the chair as she sadly repeats what Bomma says, so Bomma knows she has understood: "Someone wearing a fur collar and a hat. An old man with a walking stick. Your father . . ."

Papa is standing right beside Mama. He's concerned, his hair sleep-tousled.

"Darling . . ." says Mama.

She pauses. On the other end of the line, Bomma is still speaking.

"There's a young lady with a small girl," my mother repeats. I can hear the tears in her voice.

"It's not really happening, dear, not now. Truly. You don't have to go to Westerbork."

I've come down the stairs, forgetting to slink.

"Mother," says Mama. "You're safe. Your sister, her children, and your father aren't really there. They're not coming to get you. Honestly. You're in your own room. I'm not far away."

Mama looks despairingly at Papa.

He nods.

"I'll come," says Mama. "I won't be long."

Her hand shaking, she puts down the phone.

"You two get back to bed right now," she says when she notices my sister and me.

I hadn't heard my sister arrive. I'm a useless investigator.

It's two o'clock in the morning. Mama has gone to see Bomma.

Will she eat licorice in the car? No. It's too sad a time for licorice.

I picture Bomma in her pajamas, sitting on a platform. Around her, people are waiting for a train. A cold wind howls through the station concourse, gusting an old newspaper over the rails. A light burns behind the ticket office window, while, in the distance, a train starts to brake, its wheels squealing on the tracks.

I think about what Papa said to me, once Mama had left: "Bomma's a bit confused. It's because of the medicines she takes. Everything will be fine. Go back to your warm bed. Mama will be home soon."

Before I flick off my bedside light, I put Bessie Blue beneath my pillow. On a fresh page of my notebook, I write: *Westerbork*.

My alarm wakes me the next morning. Did I dream everything? I open my notebook. There's a new word written there: *Westerbork*.

I get up in a hurry. I can already hear Mama clattering about downstairs.

I put on my dressing gown and go down to her.

"Morning," she says.

"About last night . . ." I start off hesitantly.

"Bomma was a little confused," she says. "Things are already much better." She tries to smile, but her eyes don't laugh along.

Moz

I walk through the garden. I have to go to school.

It's misty, but the sun is shining. Dreamlight!

The shrubbery beside me stirs.

"Moz?"

I squat.

The cat meows and comes closer.

I reach out my hand, and he butts it with his head.

"Last night something horrible happened," I whisper.

Moz rolls over so I can tickle his tummy.

His soft, warm fur makes me feel happy.

How can I feel happy? Shouldn't I be worried about Bomma?

I forget to stroke Moz.

He stretches, taking my hand in his paws.

"You're right," I say. I carry on stroking him.

The red ball I found the other day lies in the damp, green grass. I kick it. Moz chases after it.

When I walk away, his green eyes follow me. But he'll soon forget me.

It makes no difference to him if I'm there or not. He plays, chases, does whatever he likes, without questioning it.

Who? What? Where? How? Why? When? Wanting to know everything is a people thing.

Consolation

I walk to school thinking about Bomma and Hesje.

I've walked this way hundreds of times before, but today it feels different somehow. My shoes seem heavier. My head feels anxious—maybe similar to what it's like in Bomma's head—a place where dark shadows lurk. But then, I also have colorful thoughts about Moz and Bessie Blue. I can feel her in my pocket. She's always there for me.

The schoolyard is crowded. I don't want to be in a crowd. Instead, I sit on the low fence beneath the tree, waiting impatiently for the bell to ring and for the school to gulp us down.

Lienke comes over. "Hi there," she says. "Have you thought of a name for our island yet?"

Together we start inventing names.

"Celebes," says Lienke.

"That's already taken," I say. "It has to be something original, made up by us. What do you think of Far Away?"

Lienke isn't so sure. "Maybe it should be a nonsense name. Something to do with plants or trees? Then it would begin with Pla . . ."

"*Platre*," I think aloud. "Or the other way round: *Trepla*."

"That's a fun name!" says Lienke. Her face scrunches up

with laugher, bringing her freckles together in a happy cluster.

I'm pleased that our island has a name.

"Oh, and . . ." Lienke checks to make sure no one is eavesdropping. "We need a plan for Saturday."

"Yes," I whisper. "We have to save the tree."

Then the school bell clangs.

I run with the autumn wind at my back. School is finished, the day is over, and it's time to go home.

"Hello!" I call, sliding open the door.

No reply.

I listen hard.

"Mama!" I call out.

Still silence.

Then I hear a quiet voice. "I'm in here."

I go into my parents' bedroom. The drapes are closed.

Mama sits on the edge of the bed. "I took a nap," she says. "I didn't sleep much last night."

"Yes, I know." I scrunch my cold hands up into my sleeves.

"Would you make us some tea?" she asks.

The water takes a long time to boil.

As soon as the kettle whistles, I murmur the words of the nursery rhyme that Mama often says: "*Cry, baby, cry.*"

I pour the boiling water over the tea leaves. "I can do that," Mama usually says, but not this time.

Carefully, I carry the teapot into the dining room.

I fetch cups and biscuits from the kitchen.

Then I go and sit opposite my mother and pour the tea, the pot shaking a little.

"Did you visit Bomma today?" I ask.

Mama looks at me and nods.

Then she looks down and I see her swallow.

"Oh, the radio's not on," she mutters. She gets up quickly, pushes the button, and sits down again. Music blares.

What's going on?

Mama sighs, rubbing her eyes. Her hand gradually slides from her eyes down to cover her mouth, as if she's said something terrible. Her eyes are red.

I stand up, go over to her, and cautiously put my arm around her shoulders.

Grilled Cheese

"How lovely that you're here," says Auntie Meirke.

There are two plates on the table.

"Sit down, sit down." Her bleached-blond hair sticks to her forehead.

She sets down two full glasses of chocolate milk.

I don't like chocolate milk, but I don't say so.

Something made from bamboo hangs on the wall above the table.

"What is that?" I point to it.

"Unusual, isn't it?" says Auntie Meirke. "We found it, my husband and I. It was on the sidewalk, just dumped there. We liked it and took it home. It's meant to be here with us, I thought. That's why we found it."

I'll have to think about that. Do you find things by chance, or is it your fate to find them?

Lienke checks out the kitchen.

"Best keep your distance from the panini press," Auntie Meirke warns her. "It's very hot."

The grilled cheese sandwiches are ready.

They aren't too bad at all.

"How are things with you, child?" Auntie Meirke asks.

Lienke hurriedly swallows a mouthful of grilled cheese. "Fine."

Auntie Meirke cups her hands around a mug of tea. "Yes, every household has its cross to bear. You simply have to live with it. Take my mother, for example. She's not well. She forgets everything—she doesn't even know who I am. Sometimes I'm scared I'll get her sickness later on, when I'm older. But what's the point of fretting about it now? There is none. Am I right?"

Lienke puts her hand under the table to feed the dachshund.

"Best not to," says Auntie Meirke. "His stomach can't cope. He's too old." Auntie Meirke laughs. Not because she's happy.

We hear a fart under the table.

"Do they trouble you at school?" Auntie Meirke nods at Lienke's hands. "Life's never easy if you're at all different. You're having another operation soon. Your mother told me."

Lienke doesn't reply.

Neither do I.

Auntie Meirke talks too much, far too much.

The dog lets another fart rip.

"Don't be strangers," says our neighbor as we leave.

We race down the garden path.

On the street, Lienke pinches her nose and we double over with laugher.

"The sandwich was really nice though," I say.

"It went down well," Lienke agrees.

Amsterdam

There's a long row of encyclopedia volumes in Papa's study.

Now's the time, I decide. Papa is out and Mama is busy in the kitchen. Feeling like a real investigative journalist, I slink downstairs.

I carefully push open the door to the study. For a second the small hallway is filled with daylight. I hurry into the room and shut the door. I go to the bookcase and select the right volume: the *W*. The book is a dark-red color with a black stripe on its spine. It's heavy. Probably because it's so full of facts. My finger flicks through the pages. *Westerbork, a town in Drenthe. Transit camp for thousands of Jews, 1 July 1942 until 12 April 1945.*

What's a transit camp? I ask myself. I keep reading: *In Amsterdam, Jews from the city had to assemble in the Hollandsche Schouwburg from where they were sent to death camps via Camp Westerbork.*

Hollandsche Schouwburg? I read these words again. I quickly select another volume: the *H*. *Hollandsche Schouwburg. Theatre in Amsterdam. From 1942–1943 an assembly place where Jews from Amsterdam were brought before being transported to Camp Westerbork.*

I hear a noise. My hands are shaking as I put the book back tidily into the bookcase. I really want to read more, but I don't want to get caught. I check for any traces of my presence I may have left behind; I even pick one of my long black hairs off the floor.

I go into the kitchen as if nothing's happened.

My mother scribbles numbers on a piece of paper. She's adding up calories for her work. If the tally's too high, then someone's eating too much.

She's very fast at counting.

"Mama," I ask as lightly as I can, "you were born in Amsterdam, weren't you?"

She looks up, surprised. "Yes, in Betondorp, a district in East Amsterdam. At first, a lot of concrete was used for building the houses. That's why they called it Betondorp: Concrete Town."

"In 1938?"

Mama nods. "Why do you want to know?"

I shrug. "Just because."

"Johan Cruijff, the famous football player, lived in Betondorp too. I saw him kicking his football against a lamppost in the neighborhood. He never missed."

My mother looks rather pleased with herself, even though she doesn't care in the slightest about football.

"Did your whole family live in Amsterdam?" I ask. "I mean, like aunts and uncles."

"Our family, yes," Mama answers carefully. "There was also some family in Scheveningen, right by the sea. But don't ask me anything else now. I have to finish these calculations."

・ ・ ・

I go to my room and update my notebook. *Transit camp. Thousands of Jews, Hollandsche Schouwburg, Betondorp, Scheveningen.*

But our family isn't Jewish, is it?

"Should we go out for an ice cream?" Mama calls up the stairs.

"Okay!" I call back, surprised.

"Two soft serves," says my mother.

A bored teenager prepares our order and soon we're strolling with two glistening ice creams to a bench in the old marketplace.

Autumn leaves quietly zigzag from the trees.

Then Mama trips. It's as if I see it happening in slow motion, even though it actually happens very quickly.

I know right then and there that I'll never forget her blanched, terrified face. With my ice-cream-free hand, I help her up. We look sadly at the remains of her soft serve on the cobblestones.

Sitting on a bench, we take turns licking my soft serve.

It's lovely and creamy

"Was there ice cream when you were young?"

Thinking about ice cream makes my mother smile. "Definitely," she replies. "How could I forget? They were a real treat. They cost three, five, or ten cents. The vendors came door-to-door with their ice cream carts. One of them was called Mr. Van Gelder—I still remember that. As far as we kids were concerned, the two ice cream men, with their gleaming white carts, were heroes. I never saw them again after the war."

"Why not?"

"They just never came back."

"But why didn't they?"

"Finish your ice cream," says Mama. "I've had enough."

The fallen soft serve has almost melted away.

Moz

It's dusk in the garden.

If I were a cat, now's the time I'd be on the prowl. Still enough light for me to see, but not enough for others to see me. *Slinkingsilentspy.*

Is he there? "Moz?" I whisper.

I listen closely.

Not a sound. Perhaps I'm wrong.

I hear a car in the distance. The call of a bird. No Moz.

"Moz! Oh," I say, "there you are. . . ."

The cat slinks by, headbutting as always.

I stroke him gently, and soon he purrs.

Cats purr, and they can cry without shedding tears.

"If only I was a cat on the inside," I sigh, forgetting again to stroke him.

Moz digs his claws into my hand.

"Ow, don't do that! Horrible cat!"

I'm not really angry. I go back to stroking him.

Moz purrs, satisfied.

"You've got no idea what is or isn't allowed. You just do whatever comes to mind."

Perhaps I should do that more often too. In other words, visit Bomma and look at the family album again!

Meow.

"Yes, that's a promise."

Scarf

"Do you want to come with me to buy a PLO scarf?" my sister asks.

There isn't a great choice of clothing stores in town. Together we cycle bike to Nieuwstraat anyway.

"Do you want one as well?"

I shake my head. I don't need one of those black-and-white checkered scarves. I prefer something more colorful; black and white is dreary.

"Have you ever seen Bomma's photo album?" I ask.

"Which photo album?"

"You know, of the family from long ago, the one with all the black-and-white photos."

"Oh, that one. The past is hard work. I don't have time for it. Mama's scared of life. Nothing's allowed. Always being careful about what you say, how you say it, when you say it. . . . Jeez, all her rules."

I look at my sister's unsmiling face.

Then I make a decision: Tomorrow I'll go to Bomma's on my own. I'll check out her photo album properly.

"Look, what do you think of this one?" my sister asks.

"Nice," I say. And it's true, the scarf suits her really well and matches her denim jacket.

My sister takes it to the cashier.

"That's a nice scarf, isn't it?" says the saleslady in a Brabant dialect.

My sister replies in the same dialect, as if she were born here. "You're so right. My mother doesn't know a thing about fashion. She didn't want me to get it. But I really, really wanted this one."

I don't have a knack for the dialect the way she does. We moved to Brabant five years ago, and I'm still a fish out of water, teased for the hard *g* of my hometown dialect, which I can never remember to shake. It's right there in the middle of my last name: Ver-ste-gggguuh-n.

At first, the teasing got to me and I lashed out without warning at those who were doing it, but not anymore. I'm not allowed. "You're far too old for that," Mama said. "You know it's not the right thing to do. Just ignore them."

I'm not really allowed to do anything. It's better not to stick out like a sore thumb. Better to keep myself under control. That can be hard, especially when I get angry and forget. But Mama reminds me.

Mama told me that after her parents moved from Amsterdam to Antwerp, she too had a hard time adjusting to the different way people spoke. She was still very young then and found it impossible to understand what people were saying in this strange new dialect.

"But," she explained calmly, "things eventually sorted themselves out."

My sister is clever to have gotten so used to the Brabantian dialect. Maybe that's why she has more friends than I do? She's always busy; she's on the hockey team, goes horseback riding, and all that. There's only five years between us, but sometimes she seems as faraway as an adult. Maybe she finds me as remote as a little kid?

"I'll tell you what," says my sister when we get home. "Mama's not home till dinnertime. Let's listen to the record that has Bompa's voice on it. It's pretty ancient, so we have to be really careful with it. It's one of a kind."

"Are we allowed to?" I ask. "What if it breaks?"

"I know where it is," she says determinedly. "I also know how to put it on. It's nice to listen to. Last time, I listened to it secretly."

I look at her with newfound respect.

She finds the record and deftly removes it from its faded paper cover.

She lays the black disk on the turntable. She pushes in a button and the record begins to spin. Carefully, she lifts up the arm of the record player and lowers the needle into the groove.

There's the sound of crackle and static, and then Bompa begins to speak. His oh-so-familiar voice fills our living room. It's amazing to hear him again, now that he's no longer here.

"He's talking about the war," I whisper.

"Not the Second," my sister whispers back.

I don't quite understand, but I don't ask any questions. I just listen.

Suddenly the glass door slides open and Mama's standing there, right in front of us.

"Out!" she says, cold as ice. "This is the last thing I want to come home to."

She looks at me. "Out of my sight."

Frightened, my sister and I turn in unison to the record player. My sister lifts the needle clumsily off the record. Bompa's voice stops right away.

Mama disappears into the bathroom and firmly locks the door.

My heart races.

It wasn't allowed, we knew that, but we did it anyway.

My sister's face has turned bright red.

Together we go upstairs. We stay there until we think Mama's bout of anger has passed.

On the Sly

Today I'm going to visit Bomma on my own. That in itself is nothing unusual, but the fact that I'm going in secret is. Today's a good day for it, since Mama's at work until five.

School's out.

"Coming around to play?" Lienke asks as we head outside.

"Can't," I mutter. "I'm going to Bomma's."

"Pity," says Lienke. "See you tomorrow then."

I bike as fast as I can to the Molenwiek.

Out of breath, I knock on Bomma's door.

What will she say? This is the first time I've gone alone to see her since she's been so ill. Will she let me look in the photo album again? Will the people she saw on the night she called my mother still be in her room? Will I be able to see them too? And, if so, does that mean the photo album has come to life? Will I dare ask who they are?

I knock again and reach for the door handle. I'm expecting to hear a "yes," but there's no reply.

I open the door very slowly and go inside.

"Bomma?"

I look around.

Bomma is sitting on the edge of her bed, naked and so very fragile.

I hurry over to her and try to cover her with a blanket.

"No," she says forcefully. "I can't stand anything."

I push the walker off to one side, but she quickly takes hold of it.

She rocks to and fro, her face grim.

"What's happened?" I ask her gently.

"I've been told off," she says, her head bowed. "The nurse told me I had to go downstairs. 'It'll be good for you,' she said, but it was terrible. The woman from next door denounced me as a Jew."

"What? What do you mean?" I ask.

Bomma is hunched so far forward it's as if she's folded in half. Everything about her seems wretched. Her eyes, mouth, lips, breasts, shoulders are all slumped with grief. Even her thin legs look inconsolable, their knees turned inward.

Should I ring Mama? No. I sit beside Bomma on the edge of the bed.

"My neighbor denounced me as a Jew," she says again.

"Mrs. Knipping? Why would she do that? Maybe she said something different and you misheard her. She wouldn't have said anything to upset you just out of the blue."

Bomma looks up at me in a way I don't recognize. I search for a word that fits the expression on her face.

"You must have misunderstood. Mrs. Knipping is nice. You can trust her."

Bomma looks right through me, her clear blue eyes fiercely intense.

They shock me into silence. Her expression reminds me of Mama.

It's dead quiet in the small room. I'm starting to feel stifled.

I have to say something—the silence is so awful. "Would you like some tea?"

Bomma nods.

As I start to get up, she takes my hand.

I stay where I am.

"It's dark in my head," says Bomma, under her breath.

Tears fill my eyes. The room blurs and becomes hazy. I haven't got any answers, only more questions. Jew. Is that a term of abuse? It can't be, can it?

A brief knock and the door opens.

Nurse Ferry comes inside. "What a glum face," he says airily. "And while your granddaughter is visiting too."

Bomma lifts her head. It's like she's finally seeing me properly. A quick smile flits across her face.

I dig my hands deep into my pockets while Ferry gives Bomma her medicines. Taking charge, he helps her into a dressing gown and sits her down in her chair. He doesn't seem to hear her protests.

Bomma peers outside.

What is she seeing now?

Hidden

Ferry and I are standing in the hallway. I look up at his moustache. It looks down at me, as earnest as his eyes.

"Perhaps it's best not to come again by yourself," he says gently. "Your oma's ill. She's on strong medications that can sometimes cause her to be confused. You're rather young to have to deal with it."

Guilt creeps up on me, and my temples start to throb. I nod.

"But . . . someone denounced her as a Jew."

The words just fall out of my mouth; I couldn't keep them inside any longer.

Ferry considers what I've said. "Your oma's had to deal with many things in her life," he says, not beating around the bush. "All sorts of experiences from the past are resurfacing now. Being Jewish during the Second World War means she went through a lot."

This is the first time anyone has talked to me like this.

"Do you discuss the past at home?" he asks.

"No," I reply.

"Try talking it over with your mother," Ferry suggests.

I bike home so fast it hurts to breathe. I don't mind that; it hides a different pain, one deep inside. Discuss things with

Mama? *How?* By just putting one word after another, until they become proper sentences with a subject and a predicate, I guess. But it's never as easy as that, because Mama never responds.

How dark is it in Bomma's head? I visualize her face in front of me. Her lips form the word *Jew.*

I didn't dare ask for the photo album. Of course not!

My family. Jews. War. It's all so much clearer now. Jews! The people who Hitler hated. The people Mr. Schouderland taught us about.

By the time my mother arrives home, the clammy sweat on my forehead has dried.

I've decided I have to be honest. If I don't mention my visit to Bomma, then Ferry might tell, or Bomma herself.

Mama unwraps daffodils and puts them in a vase. "Aren't they lovely?"

I come clean. "I've been to see Bomma."

Mama says nothing. She puts away groceries.

"She wasn't well," I falter.

Mama still says nothing.

I'm sick of the silence. Slowly, I walk away.

Even when you don't speak, you're still saying something.

I slip between the railings. My chest and hips still slide through easily.

I flee to the small bathroom on the landing.

I watch my mirror image brush away the tears. I trace the outline of my face in the mirror. My light-colored eyes stare back at me, a little sad perhaps, but still sparkling. A small face, pale skin, dark hair. Ordinary. A forehead, a jaw, a nose. Nothing special. Except it's my face. Hidden behind it are my thoughts and my stories. Including today's.

Is it a Jewish face that looks back at me?

It doesn't feel Jewish. But how does that actually feel? I have no idea.

Once in my room, I get out my moss-green notebook and collapse into my yellow beanbag, which wraps around me like a cocoon.

It's a big mystery. There are clues hidden everywhere: in people's heads, in books and photos.

You have to ask the right questions. *Who? What? Where? How? Why? When?*

But that's not all. You also have to ask the right people those questions.

My head feels like a cluttered attic with a thousand jumbled thoughts.

If my mother saw it, she would scream in despair: *You need to do some tidying upstairs!*

I already know a lot, but there's a lot more I don't understand.

I go downstairs. My mother looks tired, but at least she's talking again. She's takes the breadcrumbs out of the cupboard and says: "Would you mind unplugging the doorbell."

I turn around and walk to the hall.

Sometimes Mama doesn't want to see anyone, and even the possibility of someone ringing the bell isn't allowed.

I know exactly which plug it is and wriggle it free. If someone pressed the doorbell now, we wouldn't hear a thing. The house would remain hushed, the door wouldn't open, and the people would go away.

I'm in bed.

Papa is in his study, directly below my room, writing an article for the newspaper. He types using two fingers, hammering the typewriter keys.

Once I held a typed sheet up to the light. All the periods and commas were tiny holes. You could see right through them.

The typewriter rattles. Now and then, it stops. When that happens, Papa is thinking about his next sentence.

I'm not allowed to disturb him when he's working. But he's allowed to disturb me when I'm supposed to be sleeping.

I put in my earplugs, and the sound of hammering stops straightaway.

Saturday

Saturday is Save the Tree Day.

Lienke and I have come up with a simple plan: We'll link our arms around the tree. They won't dare chop us down along with it! It's foolproof.

I'm in the square with plenty of time to spare. We agreed to meet at eight o'clock, and we can't be late. I want to stand by this tree; it's always stood by us. So many birds play among its leaves and its top is tall enough to tickle the clouds.

What's keeping Lienke? Though, to tell the truth, I *am* here very early.

I can't wait for her to come. We'll save the tree, just the two of us! I feel a sense of pride when I think of that.

Saturday mornings are very peaceful in town, especially in this little square.

I wait and wait. Lienke doesn't come. It must be eight o'clock by now. What's keeping her?

I reach into my pants pocket. Luckily, I have my mini-best friend—wait no—she isn't there. Where's Bessie Blue? I check all my other pockets. Bessie, where are you?

This can't be happening. I search my pocket again. Empty! I can't see her anywhere in the square, so maybe she's still in my room, under my pillow.

There's the rumble of a vehicle. Are they here?

A car towing a trailer turns into the square.

Lienke! I think despairingly. Where on earth are you?

The car stops right in front of me.

Two men get out. They don't say hello. They don't even look at me.

One of then hauls out some tools. The other loosens the rope that's holding down the tarp over the trailer.

The trailer, I gather, is for the chopped-down tree parts.

I suddenly realize that I really am on my own.

I make a brave attempt. "You can't take the tree!"

"We've got work to do, miss," one of the men says. "Go and play somewhere else."

"You can't take it," I say. "It doesn't want to go. The tree . . ."

I feel stronger with the tree behind me.

"Trees don't talk." The man laughs. "You do. Now hurry up, out of our way." He checks his tools.

"No," I try again. I'm aware of how feeble I sound.

To be honest, I've given up hope. When adults get an idea in their head, that's it—you can't shake it out.

"Go away!" the man raises his voice, irate.

I touch the trunk. Dead.quiet, the tree can't do anything but wait. Hesitantly, I move a few steps away.

The men nod and point determinedly.

The ominous sound of the chainsaw slices through the silence.

I shrink back.

Lienke! I call out once more, but only in my head.

I run away. Back to our garden. The piercing sound follows me. The crashing of the first large branches. A sighing sound followed by a dull roar.

I take shelter in the climbing tree in our garden. No Lienke, no Bessie, no more tall tree.

Mama has said it many times. You can't trust anyone.

Moz

I look around the garden.

Will Moz come today?

Or will he leave me in the lurch, the way Lienke did?

And what about Bessie Blue? I've searched everywhere in the house. No sign of her.

Maybe she's just waiting for me in the classroom, in my desk drawer.

I try to remember when I last saw her.

Of course I know she's not real, but . . . I miss her.

She smelled so nice and she was always there. Maybe I lost her so that someone else could find her, someone who needed her. In that case, she won't be alone now.

I'm alone, except I still have Moz.

The trees and shrubs are silent, waiting shadows.

"Moz! Hello, dear cat." I squat and reach out my hand.

Moz slinks past me.

Where's he going?

My eyes track him. He pads over to the shrubs and stays there, staring intensely and patiently. I wait with him.

Suddenly Moz tenses his muscles, ready to pounce.

He leaps!

Sounds of fluttering panic come from the shrubbery.

"Moz! No!" But it's too late.

Moz walks away with a bird in his jaws.

I look at him in horror.

Winter in Wartime

"During the war, as soon as you heard the air-raid siren you had to find safe refuge, and fast," Mr. Schouderland explains. "The siren meant *Danger! Seek shelter!* My mother once told me about a time the siren sounded. Her next-door neighbor put a colander over her head as if it were a helmet. For protection!"

The kids in the class grin.

I can picture it now. The colander from our kitchen, red enamel with a piece missing, upside down on the head of Auntie Meirke.

Mr. Schouderland pushes his glasses into place. "Starting tomorrow, I'm going to read aloud from a book that's set during the Second World War. The book's called *Winter in Wartime*. See you all then!"

I run home. I want to go to my room and hide away in my yellow beanbag.

Bessie Blue wasn't in my school drawer either. I really have lost her. I keep imagining her somewhere else—alone in the grass, in the street gutter, on the road—and I know she'll be missing me too.

I run even faster.

"Wait!" a voice calls.

I turn around.

Lienke is chasing after me, almost out of breath.

I pause. I don't really want to stop. The disappointment of last Saturday lies between us like a great mountain of sand.

Lienke looks at me, almost pleading. "I . . . I'm . . . sorry. The tree . . ." she stumbles.

My mouth is a straight line, just like my mother's when she's disappointed in me.

"I . . . was too scared . . . too scared to watch. I . . . we couldn't have stopped it from happening."

I glare at her.

But maybe she's right. What's done is done. The tree's been cut down, chopped into pieces, and trailered away. It'll never come back. Gone forever.

My glaring face, my clenched jaw, my frown . . . I don't want to be like this, but it just happens.

Lienke eyes me hopefully, her eyes brimming with tears.

"I understand," I mumble. "Losing the tree was a horrible moment."

Lienke nods. She smiles, very tentatively. "I'm sorry," she says. "Truly I am."

It's quiet for a moment.

"I've got something for you," she says mysteriously. "My parents gave it to me. Because I had so many questions about the war."

She wipes a tear from her cheek.

"It's a book. You can borrow it. I read it very fast. Come with me? It's at home. I'll give it to you."

"I have to get home straightaway. I promised."

"It won't take long," she says.

My curiosity wins out and I go with her.

At her place, she gives me the book, wrapped in a plastic bag.

"Thanks," I say. "But I'd better go now. I have to be home on time."

I scurry through her garden, onto the street, past the small treeless square, and home. I'm only a few minutes later than usual.

Late

"Jeska!" A pale face materializes in the darkness. My mother is wearing a black dress that goes down to her ankles. The coldness in her voice, the *Jeska* instead of *Jesje*, makes me feel as if ice water is being poured down my back.

I get such a fright, my knees forget they're holding my body up. They bend and fold.

Shocked, I scrabble upright. She doesn't offer me a helping hand.

"Straight home. That's what I told you." Her green eyes blaze.

"I . . . I was over at Lienke's. Only for a few minutes."

I clasp the book, concealed in plastic, to my chest.

Mama is simmering with anger.

"Only . . . for . . . a few minutes," I stammer.

It makes no difference.

I climb the stairs to my room. I hold onto the book as if I'm shielding a living thing.

I let myself fall into my beanbag, still wearing my coat. It puffs up. With clumsy fingers, I unzip it.

Quickly, I open the plastic bag to reveal the book. The paper smells of Lienke's house.

On the cover there's a picture of a girl with a delicate smile and dark, curly hair. *Anne Frank*, it says. *The Secret Annex.*

I turn the book over to read what it says on the back: *Anne Frank, a German Jewish girl. She kept a diary from 12 June 1942 until 1 August 1944.*

My heart beats faster.

I hurriedly take off my coat.

This isn't any old story. It's a diary. Something that really happened, something seen through the eyes of a young girl. During the Second World War.

I open the book, reading a paragraph here and there.

I read about Anne, about her friends and her family. She tries to understand the world around her while she has to stay in hiding. She writes to Kitty, her imaginary friend. I'm reminded of Bessie Blue.

"Dinner is ready!" My mother's voice echoes through the house.

A bowl of steaming potatoes sits on the table, along with beans and meatballs.

Mama serves us.

My sister slides into her seat. "Potatoes again," she grumbles.

"How was school?" Papa asks, holding out his plate.

"Mr. Schouderland is going to read a special book out loud to us."

"Fairy tales?" asks my father.

"No," I laugh. "We're eleven, you know."

"What, then?"

Everyone waits for my reply.

"*Winter in Wartime*, or something like that," I say under my breath.

My sister looks at my mother. My father looks at his plate.

"Oh," says my mother. "That seems far too unsettling for young children."

And that's how it's left.

Reading Aloud

I sit at my desk, deflated. What a rotten day. I feel in my empty pants pockets and think for the umpteenth time about Bessie Blue. Where on earth can she be? Another half hour before I can go home.

Mr. Schouderland claps for attention.

"Today I'm going to spend the last half hour reading aloud from *Winter in Wartime* by Jan Terlouw." He's holding a fat, well-thumbed book. "Before I begin, I have to tell you that the story takes place during the Second World War and that it's a real nail-biter. Some of you might find it too intense."

"Not me!" Michiel calls. He pushes his chest out.

He looks like a strutting dove, one of those silly puffed-up birds that coolly stay on the road even when you're cycling straight toward them.

"There are some parents who think it's not a suitable story for their children to listen to," says Mr. Schouderland. Then he looks at me. "You may leave the class, Jeska. Other children can go with her if they'd rather."

I look at him with astonishment. I have to leave the class? Am I hearing him right?

He nods encouragingly at me. "Your mother rang."

Bewildered, I push my chair back. No one else gets up.

I feel the sting of tears. I get up as if I'm being moved by strings. Leaving the classroom has never taken so long. All eyes are on me.

Once out in the hallway I wonder: Where am I supposed to go?

And what will the other kids say to me after school? If only I was invisible or one of my failed drawings—then I could erase myself.

As soon the school bell rings, I'm the first to get my coat. I grab it and dash out, dragging it on as I walk. Get out. Don't look back. Avoid seeing classmates.

But, nevertheless, I can sense their sideways glances. Their laughing and mocking.

I hear quick footsteps behind me. Lienke's voice: "Wait!"

She links her arm with mine. "I'll walk with you!" she cries, overly cheerful.

I see Irene watching. She waves.

"What was it all about?" I ask Lienke.

She shrugs. "The first chapter wasn't too scary. It's about a boy during the war. He lives in a town. There isn't a lot to eat, and at night there's a blackout."

"A blackout?" I ask.

"Yes. So they don't get bombed or shelled, they cover their windows at night to hide the light."

I look at the ground.

"Are you coming to work on our island?" Lienke asks.

"I don't know," I say.

"Please," says Lienke.

"Maybe," I say. "Home first."

"I'll see you later then," Lienke says when we reach our street.

"There you are," says Mama as I slide open the door.

She's ready with tea and cookies.

I sit on the edge of my chair.

I don't want tea or cookies.

"And this is for you as well, for tomorrow." She places a packet of sweets on the table.

I look at it in surprise.

"For the last half hour."

I can't bring myself to say thank you.

I'm upset about what she's done. I don't feel like saying anything, so I don't. I bottle it up, knowing that even when you don't speak, you're still saying something.

"Hi!"

Lienke meets me on the street.

"Should we . . . ?" We both start talking at exactly the same time and that makes us laugh.

I feel a little lighter, now that everything seems back to normal. . . . Not that I'll forget that she left me, and the tree.

We head over to her house.

"I'm reading your book," I say.

"And?" Lienke asks.

"It's good." I reply. "She's so full of life."

Lienke kicks a stone away. "I can't believe that such terrible things happened."

"Even worse than terrible. Appalling."

As soon as we're inside Lienke's, we change the subject to Trepla, our secret island. Nothing appalling happens there, only nice things.

Jasper

It's time.

I'm ready to leave even before Mr. Schouderland picks up the book. The bag of sweets is tucked up my sleeve.

Stand up straight, I think. Shoulders back.

Hey, what's happening? I'm not the only one standing up.

Jasper takes his time, but he gets up as well.

Irene can't believe her eyes. (She's not been blue again, since that first time.)

I leave the classroom first, holding the door open for Jasper.

He laughs a little awkwardly once we're in the hallway. "My mother rang the school too," he says shyly, staring down at his large feet.

"Yesterday I went and sat in the bathrooms," I say.

He follows me there. Together we sit on the windowsill.

I bring out the sweets. "Want some?" I ask.

Jasper looks at the cone-shaped bag in surprise. He scrabbles around for some licorice cubes.

"I'm one as well," he says.

"One what?" I ask.

"You can tell from my last name: Cohen."

I don't follow. "What do you mean?"

"Jewish. But you don't have a Jewish last name," he says. "Verstegen." He sees how puzzled I am. "Cohen is a Jewish name. Didn't you know that?"

"I . . . I've never thought about it," I tell him honestly.

"Your mother must be . . ."

The door opens.

"Hey," says Lienke.

I grin at her.

I know why she's here. She's determined not to let me down a second time.

The three of us eat sweets together. The time goes by much faster than it did yesterday.

"See you tomorrow," I say to Jasper when the bell rings.

"See you tomorrow," he says.

In the schoolyard, I see Jasper pointing to me. He's talking to Erik.

Lienke nudges me. "Any sweets left?"

I let her choose. She picks out a licorice.

"I went to visit Bomma not long ago. Alone." I feel as if I'm giving away a big secret.

Lienke raises her eyebrows.

"She was very upset. It wasn't very nice."

Lienke and her freckles both look concerned. "And then?" She puts the licorice in her mouth.

"Well . . . and then I left. My mother was mad because I went by myself."

"You're allowed to visit your Bomma, aren't you?" says Lienke. "There's nothing wrong with that."

I'm happy she says that, and I ask her, "Would you go again, even if you knew your mother wouldn't let you?"

Lienke considers. "I'm not sure."

Moz

"Do you sometimes feel ashamed of yourself?" I ask Moz.

The cat ignores me.

"I doubt it," I answer on his behalf. "Cats don't blush."

They don't look back or ahead, they just live their contented cat lives until one day . . . they're gone.

Cats play with fallen autumn leaves because they blow about in the wind. They couldn't care less how the leaves got there or what it is that whirls them about.

Playing games used to be enough for me. I still remember: The days were never-ending. One minute I'd be a fairy, the next a gnome. Why are things so different now?

I play with Moz. For a while I forget everything else.

I tickle him with a blade of grass.

He tries to catch the tip of it.

Missed!

PART III

Throne

There's no one home when I get back.

There's a letter on the table.

> I have to pop in to work,
> I'll be back about dinnertime.
> Have some tea and cake, love Mama.

During the day, the house holds its breath. The furniture waits patiently for us, and not until we're all home does everything come back to life. Except for the antique chair in the living room. That dances when we're not here. I'm positive it does.

I glance at the old, dark chair. Wooden frame, upholstered in leather, with clawed feet.

No one's allowed to sit in it. No way; it's far too fragile. The leather seat is dented and torn, probably because of the heavy bottom that must have sat in it ages ago.

The chair tempts me. I've always wanted to try it out. It's like a throne.

Today's the day! I unzip my coat. My bottom hovers over the seat. Should I or shouldn't I? Yes! Slowly, I lower myself down. Air whooshes out of the cushion. "Sorry," I whisper to it.

The elegant chair is like a threadbare mountain, the torn leather bumpy and uncomfortable. Its beauty tricked me.

The phone shrills.

I leap up. Hot with fright, I pick up the phone. Is it my mother?

"Hello?"

"Where's Branc?" a voice asks.

Bomma, I think nervously, asking for Mama!

"Hi, Bomma. She's not here."

It's quiet on the other end of the line. All I can hear is the faint tremor of Bomma's fingers on the phone.

"Where's Branc?" she repeats.

"She's not here." I hesitate. "Do you want me to come?"

"Yes."

"Okay," I say. "I'm coming. Bye."

Anxious, I re-zip my coat.

My second solo visit to Bomma's without permission. But this time I have to help!

Ferry is leaving Bomma's room as I arrive.

"Here again?"

I immediately turn red with guilt.

"Things are going a little better. I sat with her for a while. She was confused, but now she's back to being a lady."

Bomma is in her chair.

"Hello," I say, giving her a kiss.

"Child, you're so cold."

I sit beside her. "Do you want some tea?"

Bomma shakes her head.

"Do you want to take a look at the family album?" I ask.

She nods.

I fetch the square book lying on the table and place it on her lap.

She opens it carefully and points to a photo I remember from before.

"This is my sister," she says. "Liesje. Isn't she lovely? My dear sister."

I look at the lady with the wavy dark hair. It's beautifully done up.

Bomma's blue eyes stare at the picture. Perhaps her sister is coming back to life in front of her?

"I miss her every day."

Her trembling fingers turn to the next pages. "These are Liesje's children. Eddy and Hesje. They were such darlings."

Eddy, who's holding his sister in his arms, has a shy smile. Their cheeks are just touching. Two pairs of dark eyes, each with their points of light, look out at us. Eddy's gaze is happy, a little unruly maybe, while Hesje's is dreamy.

"Aren't they here anymore?" I ask.

Bomma shakes her head. "Transported." Her fingertips touch the photo.

Transported. I know now what that means. Anne's diary, which I'm already halfway through, explained it. They were killed. No, an even worse word: murdered.

Back Then

When I see Bomma, I think about the small glass bird that stands in its cubby, next to the empty space belonging to Bessie Blue. I don't like to touch the bird. I'm always afraid that some part of it will break off. Its beak, maybe.

"Will you tell me about the old days?" I ask.

Bomma places her hands on the album. "Of course," she says. "Where shall I start?"

"When you were a child?" I ask.

"Your age?" Bomma asks. She strokes her chin. "It was a very long time ago. I only remember snippets of it."

"What's the first thing you remember?"

"We lived in Amsterdam. With . . . my mother, my father, and my two sisters. My father, David, was so fun loving, always ready with a joke. He sometimes pretended to be an opera star. He'd put on a long-playing record and then, with great gusto, he'd sing along to the songs that filled the room."

That makes me laugh.

"Your uncles, Dolf and Peter, doted on him. They were spellbound as they watched his sleight-of-hand tricks with a pack of playing cards.

"My mother . . . well, it wasn't easy for her. My father did what he felt like doing, while she had to sort out everything at home. She was such a lovely lady. For years after she died, on her birthday I'd place a stem of laburnum on her photo."

Bomma falls silent.

"Did he have brothers or sisters?" I ask.

"My father?" Bomma asks. She smooths a wrinkle in her dressing gown. "He was the oldest of three brothers. His youngest brother, Israël, was a writer. Emanuel was a publisher. All the talk at home was of books."

The same as now. We read a lot at home.

Bomma's face seems to relax as she talks about the past.

"One day he haunted the house with a sheet over his head. We had such a hilarious time because he was a ghost who smoked a pipe!"

I can imagine it all happening.

Bomma's face clouds over. "He was also taken by the Boche, the German soldiers, in a cattle truck. Along with his shining walking stick, his jokes, his playing cards, and his pipe."

The smile is wiped from my face.

The midday sun creeps softly into the room, as if it also wants to listen to Bomma's story. I'm reminded of when I was younger, when Bomma read *Winnie the Pooh* to me in English. But sunshine doesn't really fit this story. It's better suited to rain.

Bomma slowly turns another page.

"That abominable war," she whispers.

I look at her.

"My sisters, Esther and Liesje, shared the exact same birthday as my father."

"That's amazing," I say.

"Yes," says Bomma. "They all got presents and I didn't. I must have looked very crestfallen because my mother said: 'Go upstairs and see what you can find on the dresser in the bedroom.' And there it was—especially for me—a green pencil case, lacquered in brown, with a bird painted on the lid."

Bomma's eyes start to sparkle when she remembers this.

"I loved my mother so much. A caring, calm woman. Your mother is named after her, Branca. That used to happen in families."

"Can you tell me more about your sisters?"

"I always got on well with Liesje. As children we put on short plays and picked bouquets of flowers. Later on, my children played with hers, Eddy and Hesje.

"Your mother was the same age as Hesje. They were inseparable."

Bomma shuts her eyes as she carries on talking.

I listen as I've never listened before.

"And then, one day, Hesje was gone and she never came back. No one dared to tell Branca exactly what had happened. She was only five years old, of course. She wouldn't have fully understood, and she missed her cousin."

"Yes," I say, holding my breath.

"Your mother got Hesje's clothes after she was taken

away. Clothing was hard to come by during the war. It would have been a shame to get rid of them."

It almost sounds like an excuse.

"Your mother was a little taller than Hesje, so the clothes were too small. The bow on the dress was too high. Your mother didn't like that."

I imagine my mother as a child. Twirling in front of the mirror, just like she does today. Carefully checking how her clothes fit. She's very particular with her clothing.

Bomma's fingers search for the next pages in the album.

"Esther," she says. "My other sister."

An elegantly dressed lady with dark pinned-up hair and a baby in her arms looks back at us.

"She fell in love in the camp."

"Really?" I ask, bewildered.

Bomma straightens her glasses. "Her husband had died and she was left with two children. One day, after she'd secretly slipped outside, she was picked up by the Germans and transported to the camp. Perhaps the romance helped Esther endure those final days."

Bomma has sunk deep into thought.

I realize how clearly she's been speaking the whole time.

"I was scared even to go outside. I used my handbag to hide the star on my checkered coat." She places her hand on her chest, the left side, as if she can still feel the star emblazoned there.

What happened with Mama in the department store suddenly falls into place. The checkered jacket. My mother didn't see a bright and happy pattern—she saw war.

"We had to pay for the star ourselves, and sew it on," Bomma says, full of disgust. "That symbol."

I can see her now, needle, thread, and sewing materials gathered on her lap. Did she make impatient stitches like mine, or, like Mama, did she sew very tidy ones?

Underground

"They thought: We're going to work. They thought: We're coming back. Once there, they thought they had to have a shower, but it was a lie. Camp Sobibor . . ."

Bomma spreads her hands over the photo album as if she's seeking some comfort there.

"This is all I have left of them," she says quietly. "We have to remember them. You too."

"Yes," I whisper.

"How did you manage to survive the war?" I ask.

"By keeping quiet," says Bomma. "By staying inconspicuous. Being silent became the norm. I was safe in Betondorp for a time. Bompa wasn't Jewish. At first, Jewish women married to non-Jewish men were spared transport to the camps. But there came a time when I still had to go into hiding. 'Going underground,' it was called."

Bomma stares outside.

"We used English to discuss what needed to be done, so as not to make the children anxious. Little Branc, Stella, and Bompa all had scarlet fever. I wanted to look after them, but I had to get away. I could have been exposed by someone at any moment. It tore me apart to hear Branc wailing. I can still feel that numbness in my body, once I'd closed the door behind me."

Bomma seems to have exhausted herself, yet I don't want to stop her. I let myself be swept along by her story.

"A friend took me in until the immediate danger passed. We nicknamed her the Honorable Lady," she says. "The war finally ended. I . . . I was still here . . . the only one of my entire family still alive."

How sharply she's remembering everything, I think. The way she told her story has brought the photos to life. I can picture great-grandfather David fooling around with a ghostly sheet over his head, and I can see Bomma helping my mother—then still a child—to put on Hesje's clothes, and Hesje herself in a camp. . . .

The sound of the ringing phone gives me a fright. I leap up and take the receiver off its cradle. "Mrs. Kohnhorst-Querido's phone."

"Nicely said," says my Uncle Peter. He's one of Mama's brothers and lives in Amsterdam.

"Hello," I say.

"I'd like to talk to my mother," Uncle Peter says. "Can I? I've heard she's not doing so good."

I pass the phone to Bomma.

It's a short conversation. Uncle Peter talks more than Bomma. I hear him ask: "How is everything?" to which she gives a very brief reply: "So-so."

I realize how difficult it is to answer that particular question.

• • •

"Is there anything else I can do?" I ask once the telephone call is over.

Bomma looks tired. I get my coat.

"A drink?" I ask. "A book?" Her bookcase is overflowing, she's read so much.

Bomma shakes her head. "Just let me sit here quietly."

She folds her hands over the album again.

She isn't completely alone, I think, and I close the door behind me.

Candles

"Where have you been? Have you got a boyfriend?" My sister stands in the doorway, grinning.

I blush.

"Doesn't matter," she says. "Boys are nice. I can have a really good laugh with Paul, my boyfriend. We can be as noisy as we want. Not like here at home. With him I can be myself."

So Paul of the life-and-death letter is her *boyfriend*. Yes, it's true, I think, we don't laugh much at home. Even birthdays and other occasions are serious.

I have to smile, though, when I think of Christmas. In December there's always a tree in the room and all the decorations come out. My sister hangs her special ones on the tree and I hang mine. Papa is allowed to top it off and Mama checks that everything is well arranged.

We leave the candles for last. We must be the only family left in the world that still uses real candles. You pinch open the small candle holders and fasten them onto the branches. They're full of candle wax and pine needles from past years, which makes them tricky to open and close. The big moment—lighting the candles—comes once we've finished eating Christmas dinner.

It's hard to really enjoy the effect. Everyone is scared

and thinks: Are we going to go up in flames? But no one actually says so. There are no presents under the tree, just buckets of water. "You never know," Mama says.

My sister makes herself a sandwich loaded with ham, salad, cheese, and curry sauce. She takes it to the table to eat.

She's about to bite into it when we both hear the same sound: Mama coming up the driveway.

"Hoi, Ma," says my sister, her mouth stuffed with sandwich by the time my mother slides open the door.

Don't talk with your mouth full, I predict.

And yes, Mama doesn't let us down: "Don't talk with your mouth full."

When my mother joins us with a cup of tea, my sister says to her, "Ma, I've been meaning to ask you—can we eat something other than potatoes and gravy all the time? Rice maybe, or spaghetti once a week, say?"

As always, my mother frowns.

She doesn't answer immediately.

"My taste buds are so bored," my sister goes on. "They're desperate for something different."

"Spaghetti isn't healthy," says Mama. "Potatoes with vegetables. They're part of a balanced diet."

I escape upstairs before an argument begins.

Now and again, I stick my head out my bedroom door to listen. The spaghetti debate is ongoing.

"I think . . ." shouts my sister.

"You should listen . . ." my mother yells back.

They go back and forth a lot, but in the end my sister wins the argument. We can have a change of menu once a week. But my sister will have to prepare it.

I'm thirsty. I cautiously make my way downstairs.

"And what are you going to ask for?" my mother snaps when she sees me.

I shake my head. Nothing at all.

That evening, I lie in bed and read some more of Anne's diary.

Bomma's story plays on and on in my head. It makes the diary even more real. It's as if I can see Bomma, Hesje, and all the other family members slipping past in the background.

Uncle

From the kitchen window, I see a red sports car pull up in front of our house.

Is that Uncle Dolf's car?

This brother of Mama's lives in London; we don't see him very often. The last time was at the family get-together. But because Bomma's unwell, he's come to the Netherlands.

A polished black leather shoe is the first thing to emerge from the car, followed by smart, dark blue, sharply creased trousers. My uncle is slim, going gray, and he has an infectious laugh.

He and Mama are so different from each other. At his house, the drapes stay open during the day; he enjoys the daylight.

"Hello," he says when he comes in. Every Dutch word he says carries a lilt of English.

Coffee is brewed before the conversation turns to Bomma; Uncle Dolf's wife, Clara; and his work. I'm surprised Uncle Dolf stays as slim as does, since he wolfs down as many biscuits as Bompa once did.

I stay in the background, listening to everything that's being said.

My sister flicks through a magazine.

Uncle Dolf gets up and looks out the window. "Clara and I enjoy gardening. Mind if I take a look around your garden?"

The telephone rings and my father snatches the receiver. *The paper*, he mouths to us, his lips forming the words without making a sound.

"Show your uncle the new path and the borders," my mother says to me. "I'll tidy up here and get things ready for lunch."

I push my chair back.

A little while later we're sitting on a garden seat beneath our tall tree.

"It's such a peaceful garden," says Uncle Dolf.

I agree, then decide to dare a question. "You lived through the war," I say hesitantly. "Can you tell me about it?"

Uncle Dolf turns to me in surprise. "What do you want to know?"

"Were you the same age as I am now?"

"A little older," says Uncle Dolf. "I was thirteen when the war began. I remember that day very well. A convoy of Dutch army vehicles drove down the street. At the front was an officer with a drawn revolver. I thought that was very exciting. The radio was on the whole day, so we could stay up to date with the latest news. At first it all seemed like a big adventure, but we soon learned that it was anything but. There were all sorts of shortages, and food became rationed. Being thirteen, I was keen to go outdoors, but I had to stay inside a lot. Helping look after the younger kids, exchanging things to get food for the family. I could sense my parents' tension."

"Where was my mother?" I ask.

"Your mother was still young when the war began. She often hid under the table because she was frightened. There wasn't much time to comfort her either; we were all too busy surviving."

It's funny; I also like hiding under the dining table. But not because of a war.

"One day we were out in our garden," Uncle Dolf says. "Bomma, me, and Branc. She was around six. She was captivated by the sight of a daffodil. She thought the sun had fallen out of the sky, that's how wonderfully yellow she thought it was. But my mother, your bomma, said: 'It only reminds me of the yellow star.'

"Then the air-raid siren went off, ear-splittingly loud. Any joy we got from that daffodil was gone, whoosh, just like that. Mother hauled Branc out of the garden and we ran inside for shelter. The whole lot of us, sardined in a tiny, dark laundry room. We held our breath until the alarm was over. I can still see the fear in Branc's eyes. Sometimes it seems as if it's never gone away."

Uncle Dolf gazes into the distance. "There's something else I remember," he says. "The card I received from my opa, David Querido, from Westerbork. All the mail from the camp was heavily censored. You couldn't just write what you wanted—that was too risky. He'd drawn a fat line under 20 August, which gave away the real reason for the letter: my birthday."

Uncle Dolf frowns. "When Bomma had to go into hiding, it became my job to take the photos of her out of our albums and burn them. It had to look as if she didn't exist anymore. If the Germans had found them, it might have spelled danger for us. I was young then and hated the job, but I knew it had to be done. Anything to protect my mother and our family."

He stops. It's a good thing no one can hear my cartwheeling thoughts.

"Bomma thought I was Hesje," I tell him.

Uncle Dolf links his fingers together. "Her mind's occupied with those days. She tries her hardest to keep everyone safe in her thoughts. I suspect that's the reason she made the photo album. Have you seen it? It's a kind of homage to them. And it helps her deal with the guilt over being the only one of her family who survived the Holocaust."

"Lunch is ready!" my mother calls.

Egg

A night full of dreams. In the morning, I rub my head to try and wake up. Bomma, Hesje, Bessie Blue, Anne—all my recent discoveries, everything I've learned, made their way into my dreams.

As soon as I lift my legs out of bed I know that today will feel like walking through molasses.

I spill my glass of water. I find a hole in my sock. And where are my hair ties?

Drat!

If only I still had Bessie Blue.

Should I buy a new friend at the toy store? I count up my pocket money. I don't have enough. Should I borrow some small change from the Tally Table in the hall? Definitely not. That's not allowed. Because nothing is.

Bessie Blue . . . Anyway, I only want her, not a new doll.

As I head downstairs, I don't say good morning. I don't say anything at all. I'm not in today. The word *Closed* is written on my forehead, invisible but evident.

I eat a sandwich and drink some tea.

"Is everything okay?" my mother asks.

No, I think.

. . .

In the schoolyard Lienke says, "Hello."

I nod, but don't reply.

We sit next to each other.

Lienke and I understand each other well enough without words.

The bell rings.

I go inside.

Staying silent isn't so noticeable in class.

"Jeska," says Mr. Schouderland, "what is the capital of Denmark?"

Unless, of course, you're asked something. Then you have to reply. Or not?

I know the answer. Copenhagen.

I just look up at him.

"No? Perhaps Michiel can tell us."

"What?"

"What's the capital of Denmark?"

"Stockholm!"

That's wrong.

Lienke raises her hand.

It's a great strategy, saying nothing. I'm happy with it. I'll try it for the rest of the day.

When the bell rings, Mr. Schouderland calls me over.

"Is everything all right?" he asks.

I just look at him.

He straightens his glasses.

"Go outside and play," he says at last.

I leave the classroom.

· · ·

"Do you want some tea?" my mother asks when I come home.

I push my cup forward without saying a word.

"Enough now," says Mama. "What a mood you're in today. They should have warned us in the newspaper that the weather was changing."

She turns and goes to the kitchen.

She comes back with an egg.

I'm really confused.

She places it carefully into the palm of my hand. "I hate wasting food," she says, "but needs must. Go outside and smash it. When you come back inside, your bad mood will be gone."

I just stare at her.

Smash an egg?

I don't think I've ever stood in the garden holding an egg.

It's a nice enough egg; it has a satisfying shape. It feels fragile and strong at the same time. And it feels cold. Perhaps the way the chill of anger feels.

I don't want to be cold on the inside.

Tears sting my eyes.

I'd rather be warm.

Maybe anger isn't the real problem?

Am I just sad?

The egg feels a little less cold.

I'm allowed to smash it.

I have to smash it.

I want to smash it.
I raise my arm.
I hesitate, and then I throw it.
The egg splatters onto the tiles.
It sounds the way it looks.
The shell is in pieces, the yolk broken.

Books

I want to get away. Away from home.

I'd rather escape the thoughts inside my head, but that's impossible. Although reading a book is a kind of escape. . . . Except not Anne Frank's diary. That's very real.

"I'm going to the library!" I yell from the garden, through the open door.

My mother calls back. "Good, don't forget your library card."

As soon as I open the door, the smell of books and stories hits me.

The children's section is upstairs. It's a big, friendly loft space with small windows. There are soft, colorful cushions scattered everywhere, where you can start reading the book you want to borrow, a story that makes you happy, one that will sing to you from your bedside table: *Read me now! Read me now!*

I climb upstairs. I choose an old favorite, *Abeltje*, a lovely book to escape into. I'd love to travel in a flying elevator the way he does.

I wait in line with the other book borrowers. "Hello," I say when my turn comes.

The librarian looks at me critically over a pair of

half-moon glasses. Or do I just imagine that? She stamps the card.

Now it's time to become an investigative journalist again. I hatch a plan.

Once I've stuffed my book into my backpack, I pretend I'm about to leave the library. I stop to flick through brochures, and as soon as the librarian is busy stamping again, I slink off to the adults' section.

I wander between rows of stark, white bookshelves. The children's section is so much friendlier. I decide I'll always read children's books.

After a careful search, I eventually find the history section.

"Bingo!" I mutter. I pull a book off the shelf: *The Second World War in the Netherlands*.

I kneel down and lay the book on my lap. There are lots of photos inside. The photos show so much destruction—I can't work out how people managed to find their way through the ruins. I see pictures of children sitting on piles of trash as if they're sitting on chairs in a classroom, listening to their teacher. Long lines of thin people waiting outside a butcher's shop. A large airplane flying scarily overhead, dropping bombs. A sign at the entrance to a park reading: *Jews Forbidden*. They weren't even allowed to go to the park!

Germans with helmets and rifles hustling people into cattle trucks.

Later in the book, there are such dreadful pictures that I

want to push the book away as if it's caught fire. *Sobibor Concentration Camp*, the caption reads.

"What are you up to?"

"I, um . . ."

A man bends down, takes the book away from me, and, shaking his head, returns it to the shelf. "Why don't you go and play outside. You'll have plenty of time for this grown-up stuff later on."

I get up and flee the library, taking shelter on a bench under the tree that stands guard in the marketplace.

"So-bi-bor," I repeat slowly.

Bomma also mentioned that name.

It feels like the photos have told me more than all the words I've heard so far. Bomma's family, Mama's family . . . in that camp.

It seems as if one question always leads to another—the more I learn, the less I understand. I'm reminded of a little verse.

> *The more I learn,*
> *the more I know.*
> *The more I know,*
> *the more I forget.*
> *The more I forget,*
> *the less I know.*
> *So, why should I learn?*

Wonder Bag

"We have to go," says Mama. "Otherwise it'll get far too busy in the city."

"That's right," says my father, deep in thought. He's engrossed in a newspaper article.

Mama sighs.

As soon as I've outgrown my jacket, my shoes start pinching. That means I need new ones—and I have to tag along to Eindhoven.

I color a section of my paper with charcoal. The noise it makes is like chalk screeching on a blackboard.

"Stop it!" my mother exclaims.

I stop immediately. I spread out the black color with my fingers. The night becomes a little less dark.

My sister, who's just coming down the stairs, quickly assesses the situation and says: "I'm not going. I have plans with a friend."

I examine my charcoal fingers. If my feet could just go to the store by themselves, the rest of me could stay home and draw.

"Damnation! Where are my keys?" Papa shouts. He already has his coat on.

Mama helps look for them. "Perhaps they're on the Tally Table in the hall?"

Key crisis.

I quickly wash my hands.

Papa parks the car.

As we get out, people walk by speaking German.

"Boche," my mother mutters.

In silence we walk across the zebra-striped crosswalk into the main shopping street.

Papa goes into a wine store while Mama and I head for the shoe store. We'll meet later at Kluijtmans, a classy cafe selling cakes and pastries.

I hate buying shoes.

It takes a long time to become friends with a pair of shoes. They start off as complete strangers, causing blisters.

With a face that could bring about a hundred years of bad weather, I confront a row of shoes.

"This pair?" asks my mother.

I shrug.

"What do you think of them?"

A shop assistant comes over. "May I help?"

"Yes, please," says my mother. "Can you take her shoe size?"

"Of course."

Not long afterward, we're outside again.

Because my old shoes were really far too small, I'm already wearing the new ones, a boring black pair with a strap over the instep.

The city's busy. I watch people talk animatedly to one another. No one seems very interested in the window displays. As far as I'm concerned, they're more interested in looking at me and my shoes. The shoes still feel foreign to my feet and the straps are already starting to chafe.

Mama and I are almost at Kluijtmans.

There's a crowd of people in 18 Septemberplein, a historic square in the city. Mama tries unsuccessfully to find a way around them.

She grips my hand, clutching her Wonder Bag in her other hand.

"It's even busier than usual," she says. Her shoulders are raised and her back is bent, almost as if she's trying to make herself look smaller.

I like Kluijtmans. The glass cabinets are full of colorful cakes with creamy white centers.

We find an empty table and order coffee and tea.

I see Papa arrive and wave him over. His face resembles mine: thunder and lightning.

"My glasses!" he yells at the top of his voice. "I dropped them." Papa takes the broken glasses from his nose and gives them to my mother.

"Shush, not so loud in here," she hisses. She examines the glasses. "The arm's almost come right off."

Mama puts her bag on the table and pokes around inside. She magically produces a roll of tape. It doesn't take her long to secure the arm to the rest of the frame. "It's only a temporary fix," she murmurs.

My father takes the glasses and puts them back on. "This table wobbles," he remarks, irritated. With both hands he seizes the edge of the table and rocks it to and fro. The cups dance dangerously.

"It's this leg," my father says.

Mama rummages in her bag again. "Perhaps this will help."

A Greek coin, left over from a past vacation, steadies the table.

We drink in silence.

My mother keeps looking outside. It's getting busier in the square. "We'll have to leave soon," she says.

"They're on strike," says my father. "They've come here to demonstrate." He looks at them with interest. "They'll make tomorrow's *Eindhoven Daily*."

"Not the paper where you work?" I ask.

"I don't think so," he replies. "This is local news."

"We really need to go," says my mother urgently, her eyes wide and watchful. She's on the edge of her chair, ready to take off.

Papa pays the bill.

"Let's go the long way around," says Mama as we stand outside.

"There's no point doing that," says my father. "It's not far to the car."

My mother isn't convinced.

My new shoes bite. Should I ask for Band-Aids? They're bound to be in Mama's bag too.

We make our way through the crowd.

My mother reaches for my hand, holding it tightly. Too tightly. The color has drained from her face.

Warily, we worm our way through the mass of people.

Mama is so scared.

And suddenly, so am I. Something, I can't explain what, takes hold of me. It feels horribly uncomfortable, like a fingernail bent backward.

I try to distract myself by counting the blobs of chewing gum on the tiles, but that doesn't help.

If only Mama had something in her Wonder Bag to deal with fear.

Moz

Moz approaches, his tail proudly in the air.

"Hi, Moz," I whisper. "How was your day? I got new shoes. And I was scared."

Moz falls playfully onto his back.

I stroke his stomach. It's so soft.

"You smell like autumn."

Moz purrs.

Suddenly, we hear the sound of a motorbike accelerating.

We're both on guard: Moz is quickly on all four paws, while I leap upright.

"It's okay," I say to reassure Moz and myself.

I begin to sing a lullaby.

Moz listens carefully before lying down again.

I scratch his soft skin, hear his purring, and let the scent of the evening wash over me.

Scars

"Are you going to wear that?" Mama asks as I come down the stairs.

I turn around and go back up. It wasn't really a question.

Of course, I could just have said "yes." After all, what does it matter if you wear black and brown together? But then it would become a discussion, and I can't be bothered with that.

Back in my room, I change into a dark-blue sweater and jeans. Blue is a safe color. I sink into my beanbag and read some more of Anne Frank's diary.

I don't go downstairs again until I hear Mama go into the bathroom.

Papa's head is deep in world news. His paper lies open on the table.

"Good that your glasses are fixed," I say, resting my arms on the Chopping Block.

"It was lucky that Mama had tape in her Wonder Bag," he says.

I nod. "She's got loads of stuff in her bag."

"Enough to survive a war," my father says in an offhand way. His thoughts are on an article about the fighting in Lebanon.

"Papa," I ask, "the two of you went through the war, didn't you?"

He looks up from the paper, taken aback. "Yes," he says. "We were still young. I don't have many memories of it. But it was a difficult time. Especially for your mother."

"Why was that?" I ask.

Papa hesitates. "Mama still grieves about that time. She prefers not to talk about it."

"About the war?"

"About all the things that happened to her family." He chooses his words carefully. "If you experience something as earth-shattering as that, it stays with you. Even small things can bring it back. Some memories are like scars."

I'm not sure I understand. "Like scars?"

Papa nods. "If you cut yourself badly, you can be left with a scar, even when the wound's healed. It can be the same when you experience terrible hardship: the memory of it becomes the scar."

"Not all memories though, right?" I ask.

My father agrees.

"So when do you notice it's become a scar?"

Papa ponders. "It's not really a visible scar. And yet, in another way, it is. . . ."

I wait for him to explain.

"Mama likes to have the drapes closed, for instance, even during the day."

That's true, I think. Even when the sun isn't shining into the room.

"She can use them to shut out the world when the world gets to be too much for her."

My fingers glide over the notches in the old tabletop. "These are like scars," I say. "Can it be like that in your head?"

Papa touches the weathered wood. "I guess you could say that. Animals used to be killed on this table. The knife slashes will always be part of the wood."

I pull my arms away from the tabletop. "Animals died on here?"

My father looks at me in surprise. "You knew that, didn't you? That's why we call it the Chopping Block."

I shrink back and try to empty my head of what I've just heard.

Why didn't I realize that was the reason for the name? I hate the table now. I'll never draw on it again.

Papa leans over his newspaper and calmly carries on reading.

I breathe the outside air and wander off to nowhere in particular. Thoughts are racing around my head like bumper cars.

In the shopping district, I nearly crash into someone. I move left and so does he. I move right; he goes right as well. We share an embarrassed kind of laugh. I decide to stand still—he can go first—and after that it's all smooth sailing.

I rest for a while on a bench. Look at that—a heap of

elastic bands, large ones. Perhaps a mailman dropped them. I pick them up and put all of them in my coat pocket, except for one, which I hold in my hand. I imagine using this one to catapult paper pellets in class. I stretch it out as far as it goes. Then I thread the elastic around my fingers, like a twisting line.

A memory comes back to me. Something my mother occasionally says about me because I'm limber: "You're like elastic!"

That memory makes me smile.

Flu

This morning I wake up with aching muscles. I'm cold but feel warm to the touch.

"Flu," says my mother. "You're staying home."

My bed is like a nest. I bury myself in the blankets. Lucky that I don't have to go to school! A shame that I'm sick.

"Drink lots," says Mama. She places a cup of instant lemonade nearby and softly closes my bedroom door.

I shiver and feel tired. I feel myself slowly drifting into a feverish dream.

I jolt awake. My body is clammy with sweat. I push back the sheets and blankets.

In my dream, I was being pursued. And I know why: The book by Anne Frank haunts me. I want to finish it, but, on the other hand, I don't. I want to know what happens, but I don't want to find out. I've had the book for ages now. I have to finish it—then I won't have to hide it in my room anymore. I take the diary from its secret hiding place.

Anne Frank is an ordinary girl in an extraordinary situation. She writes so naturally, so realistically. I hear her footsteps when she walks, the scratching of her pen on the paper, the creaking-shut of the door to the secret annex.

Anne grumbles at her parents and her teachers. She sees things, feels things. But among the "everyday" things are sentences that reveal how things around her are changing. They're only allowed to go to a Jewish hairdresser. They can't be out on the streets between eight o'clock at night and six in the morning. They can't even go to the swimming pool or the movies; everything is too dangerous.

She writes about how she's growing up and how her body is changing. She's different from me: She's open and I'm closed.

If only I could talk with someone about the book. Right now, at this very moment.

Bessie Blue. I miss her so much. I feel under my pillow where she always used to lie, but what's the point?

I've always talked to myself and always gotten an answer. Mr. Schouderland calls me a daydreamer. But my fantasies are nothing more than a limber brain stretching out in lots of different directions.

My daydreams belong to me, not to anyone else, not even to Mama.

Now and then, horribly realistic things lumber into my head like overweight elephants, impossible to push away. Maybe I have to make believe that I'm super strong.

I lie there thinking about Hesje, about Bomma, about the dreadful things that happened during the war.

I've had enough of being in bed.

I put Anne Frank's book back in its hiding place.

Do I hear a sound in the kitchen? I get up and creep down the stairs.

My mother is slicing green beans into tiny diamond shapes. Their fresh aroma lingers in the kitchen.

"Feeling better?" she asks.

I nod.

Book

"Thanks," I say. I return Lienke's book, wrapped in the same plastic bag she had wrapped it in when she gave it to me.

"Finished it?"

"All of it."

Lienke bites her lip. "Sad, isn't it?"

"The end . . . Anne's last sentences."

"Yes," says Lienke.

We fall silent.

"Should we play tag?" Lienke asks.

"Tag?"

"Yes! There's Veerle," Lienke says, beckoning to Veerle, who is across the street. "She'll play with us!"

Lienke drops the book on the curb and tries to tag me, but I'm too quick.

She tags Veerle instead, who squeals with excitement.

We run, and laugh, and yell loudly when we're tagged.

It feels wonderful to run wild like this. Free!

Then I see my mother coming out of our driveway, straight toward me.

The look on her face quickly drains the glee from mine.

"Are you crazy," she says curtly. "Your noise is drowning everything out."

I nod, holding my breath.

I disturbed her. I was too loud. Too loud is not allowed. I know that. Don't be conspicuous. Having fun meant I briefly forgot.

I look at her.

I'm not having fun anymore.

I join Anne Frank on the curb. I love books and stories because the people on the page can't interrupt you, or be interrupted by you.

I look up at my friends, who are still running about.

Lienke hurries over. "Aren't you playing anymore?"

I shrug.

Veerle calls: "I have to go home, see you tomorrow!"

"See you tomorrow!" Lienke calls back. She turns to me. "Let's finish Trepla!"

"Yes, okay," I say. And suddenly I'm longing for our island. A place where everything is allowed.

It's finicky work, but we've carried on with it, an hour here, an hour there. Now the island is almost finished.

We've made palm trees out of matches; shaped a small waterfall using some shiny, silver pieces of Christmas garland; and formed a path.

"We still need a little lake," says Lienke.

Our island is a wonderful place.

And then the moment comes. I can hardly believe it: The island is finished.

"Wow," says Lienke.

"Our island!" I say.

"You bet," she says.

There's still a map to draw, and . . .

"I'm having an operation tomorrow," Lienke says, out of the blue.

I look at her with shock.

"It has to be while I'm still growing. The scar tissue's become hard. It doesn't stretch anymore." She shows me her hands. "I'm allowed to sleep in my parents' big bed when I get home."

"Put our island beside the bed," I say. "Then you'll dream about its caves and waterfall and all its palm trees."

"I like that," says Lienke.

"I'll come and visit as soon as I'm allowed to," I promise her.

"Good." Lienke looks at her hands. "Do you know how this happened?"

I shake my head.

She hesitates and then shares her secret. "I put my hands on the hot oven when my mother was looking the other way. Just for a second."

Map

I've asked Papa for an atlas. I'm hunting for an island to use as a template for our map. Here!

In front of me lies a sheet of paper that I transformed into parchment using a tea bag.

It's dry and ready to be turned into a map.

A little while ago I couldn't have cared less about atlases, but now I love them.

My eyes trace the line of a mountain range that looks like the backbone of a giant deer.

Everything has a name, even the tiny harbor. I look closely at this island in the Mediterranean Sea.

My finger slides over the map.

People live there—children who grow up! I carry on paging my way through the world, imagining children everywhere. So many! Who knows what sort of experiences they're having right now? But, like me, they're all growing up. No child can stay a child forever.

I feel my stomach clenching. Hesje was a child, and she wasn't able to grow up . . .

What would she have thought of Trepla? Beautiful, I bet.

I imagine how a conversation with her might go.

• • •

Hesje points to the mountain top. "Can I climb up there as well?"

"Of course!" I reply enthusiastically. "And afterward, we'll paddle in the bay and stand under the waterfall."

"Is my cuddly pony allowed?"

"Definitely," I say. "But what's the very first thing you'd do if you were on the island?"

Hesje considers. "Eat an ice cream."

I draw the map and daydream about trees that grow sweets, shrubs with flowering stories, climbing plants that hug you with their leaves. A lot of animals live on the island: zebras and cute, waddling penguins.

I take the map, together with a mandarin and a packet of licorice, to Lienke's house.

I knock.

Her mother waves me inside. "She's in our bed. Come on in." She leads the way.

Lienke looks so small in her parents' big bed.

"Hi," she says with a faint smile. She raises one hand, wrapped in a thick bandage.

"I've made something for you," I say. I roll open the map for her.

"That's amazing," she whispers.

Heads together, we study the map. I drink lukewarm tea from a mug while Lienke drinks lukewarm tea through a straw.

• • •

When I get home, the house smells different. My sister won the spaghetti debate, so she's cooking! No potatoes tonight, no beans.

She glimpses me from the kitchen. Her glasses have slipped down to the tip of her nose, and her cheeks are rosy. "Ha, there you are! Could you set the table?"

Bomma

All the leaves except for one have fallen from the tree in our garden. When will the last one fall?

Even though I'm now easy to spot in the climbing tree, no one's discovered me yet.

I have a view of the whole street. An abandoned shoe lies a little way down. Shoes belong in pairs. Perhaps right now the owner is hopping around on one foot. Will they look for their lost shoe or hop straight to the shoe shop for a new pair? Or will they decide to go around with bare feet forever, to save themselves the blisters?

A newspaper sticks out of a mail slot, like a tongue poking through the front door.

My name echoes through the quiet garden.

"What is it?" I call.

My mother sees me and beckons.

By the time I've climbed down the tree, she's already back inside. I open the sliding door.

Mama sits at the table, together with my sister and father. I sit in my usual place, next to my mother.

Before anything's been said, I already know: Something's happened to Bomma.

"What is it?" I say.

"It's Bomma," says Mama. "She's . . . she's . . ."

A tremor of fear passes through my body.

One of the worst things I can imagine has happened. Being worried about Bomma isn't necessary anymore; it's not possible anymore either. Worry belongs with hope, and that's gone now.

I take Mama's hand.

She squeezes mine before she sits up straight and says: "I have to call my brothers and sisters."

It seems like such a long time ago that I was outside. A whole lifetime, even though it was just a few minutes ago.

I stare at the leafless tree and the leaves on the ground. If there were numbers on them, like on the leaves of a book, then I'd know exactly which one was the very last.

Goodbye, Bomma. A couple of days ago, you gave me a kiss. I didn't know then that it would be the last one.

Where are you now? Somewhere, or nowhere? Is Hesje there as well, and your sister, and Bompa?

You're in my head. That's where I'll keep you close.

Where exactly in the head are memories kept? I make believe a nice room with royal-blue wallpaper and a stylish lamp that emits a warm light. Along with other nice things, I'd keep my memories there: Moz, Bessie Blue, good books, flowers, the spring, colors, and now, of course, Bomma as well.

I think about *fotsekaporre*: the best word ever for a person's peculiarities.

Meow. A small black head appears.

"Moz! Where did you spring from? Did you know I needed you?"

I squat and stroke the black cat. He curls around me.

"You've come to comfort me."

Moz lets himself fall and roll though the leaves.

I gather a handful and toss them into the air. He leaps up to meet them as they spin down again.

I laugh and I play. I play and I weep.

Firethorn

"Hello?"

"Hello, Jes, can you hear me?"

It's my sister. "I can, but not very well."

"I'm in a phone booth! The wind's howling around it!"

Of course that's what the noise is. In my imagination I see my sister wind-whirling past me in the phone booth.

"I'm sleeping over at Karlijn's because the weather's so bad."

"I'll just get Mama," I say.

My mother is okay with it. Nothing else eventful happens that evening. We eat, my parents watch the news, I shower and go to bed early.

In bed, I hear the wind crashing around the house. Now and then, it makes a shrill, whistling sound.

Maybe tomorrow morning I'll wake up in England, our house and everything around us having blown across the North Sea, landing in Great Britain. I fall into a deep sleep.

Papa pulls the drapes open the next morning.

Daylight floods the room, and right away, I can tell that something's changed.

"How can that be?" my father exclaims.

Mama comes to look. "What happened?"

The three of us gawk out the window.

The tall firethorn that grows in front of the house has fallen over. The huge climbing plant is so sadly bent over that it looks as if it's given up hope. Flame-red berries are scattered everywhere, and greedy birds are gobbling them up. For them, it's party time!

Not for my parents.

"Must be because of last night's storm. How on earth will we get it back into place without the thorns scratching us to pieces?" my mother asks.

My father straightens his glasses. "I'm not sure we can even get past it."

"I know what to do!" I say.

I go outside and very carefully manage to edge past the huge plant. Being small comes in handy sometimes. Every now and then a thorn snatches my coat, as if the firethorn is trying to hold me back, pleading: "Don't go, please help me!"

"Careful!" my mother calls.

From the shed I get two long rakes. I put one rake under the top of the plant and heave it up. I can just manage the weight of it.

My father comes outside and helps with the second rake.

Berries rain down on us. I start to giggle.

Robins are the most daring of daredevils: They wolf down the berries before the blackbirds even know what's happening.

Papa and I push the plant back into place.

"Now we have to find some way of keeping it there," my father says. "Do we have anything to tie this monster up with?"

"I've got some big elastic bands in my coat," I say triumphantly. "I found them in the street."

Mama also helps.

We tie the firethorn up together—but I was the one who figured out how to do it!

Task

In my room I flick through my notebook with the moss-green cover. I couldn't keep up with the neat handwriting, so I've ended up with chicken scratch again.

But at least I know a whole lot more of my family's story. The questions helped me to find answers.

I still don't understand everything. Perhaps I never will.

I hear my mother call for me: "Can you do me a favor?" She looks at me inquiringly.

I wonder what it is she wants.

"It's a big task for a young girl," Mama says. "But you're sensible. You proved that with the firethorn, and it would be a great help to me."

She gets a notepad and a ballpoint pen. "Will you go and write down everything that's in Bomma's room?"

"Everything?" I ask.

"Yes, absolutely everything. That's very important," says my mother. "It's for my brothers and sisters. They'll be able to mark which of Bomma's things they want to have."

"I'll do it," I say, and I take the empty notepad. I put the pen in my pants pocket. I get my coat and off I go.

. . .

Reminders of summer show up here and there. Plants still in flower pots but long past blooming; a forgotten beach-bucket in a sandbox.

The autumn wind blasts straight into my face. It's a very inquisitive wind; it looks inside my ears, blows wildly through my hair, and tries to find a way into my warm coat.

I feel my cheeks glow with the cold. Winter is on its way. I'm on my way to the Molenwiek with an assignment—but just as me this time, not as a journalist.

The nursing home stands there as if nothing's happened. The clock ticks on. Everything should have come to a standstill. Even if it had been for only two minutes. Just like on Remembrance Day, a day my mother never misses. We remember along with her, but now I know why.

I pause before I open the door of the room. I recall the time that Bomma told me about her family. I was so lucky that she was still able to tell me. I take a deep breath. I have to help Mama. It's do or die. She's given me this task for a reason, hasn't she?

The room still smells of Bomma. A potpourri of coffee, soap, and talcum powder.

The daylight in the room is the same as always. Yet everything looks different, sad, as if the objects in the room know that their owner is never coming back.

Over the chair lies a cloth, an antimacassar. I know that's what its name is. Bomma told me. It's an old word.

I open the cabinet opposite the kitchenette. Face cloths. I count ten. Hand towels. Bomma's name embroidered everywhere in red thread: *Estella Kohnhorst-Querido*. I take the pen from my pocket and list one thing after the other on the notepad's pale-blue lines.

The bronze statue, the vases, the unfinished knitting. Oops, I've pulled on the wrong thread, and now it's unraveling! I'd better not write that down.

The bedside cabinet has one drawer, which I pull open. Between old keys, a pen, a handkerchief, and some loose pills lies . . . Bessie Blue!

"So that's where you are," I whisper with a sigh. I look fondly at her. "You've been a little friend for Bomma."

Does Bessie Blue have to be added to the list? No, she doesn't. Lovingly, I return her to my pants pocket.

Silver chocolate-serving tray, porcelain thimble with roses, old wooden sewing reels, pins and needles, knee-high stockings, and a half-empty pot of Nivea cream. Well, Mama wanted me to write everything down.

I fill one page after another.

I open the doors of the next cabinet. For a moment I freeze—there it is, the photo album. I was so eager to see inside it. Now I can look at it at my leisure. I kneel down and lay it carefully on my lap. It still feels as if I'm not actually allowed to do this. The album creaks as I open it. There they are again: black-and-white photos glued to the thick paper. Once more the faces of long ago look back at me.

Now I know their names. They are still strangers but known strangers.

The small girl laughs shyly. Little stars twinkle on her cardigan. She clutches a checkered, cuddly, stuffed horse to herself. Under the photo is written: *Hesje Jas-Querido, born 15 May 1938, died 11 June 1943, Sobibor.*

Photo album, I write in the notepad.

Moz

On my way to the nursing home, the notepad was empty. Now the list of things takes up half the space. I've even managed to write neatly.

I bike home. Tears prick my eyes. This time I take a different route, via the market. Over the cobblestones, past the library, the tree in the square, the music chapel, past the bench opposite the ice cream stall, via Nieuwstraat, home.

"Don't forget them," said Bomma. No, never! I'll remember everything. It's all a part of me now. Who Bomma was, who my mother is, and who I'll be—all the things that have happened tie us together like a thread in a piece of knitting. Or maybe like a cut on the tabletop, a groove in my brain, a new scar in my memory. By thinking about it often, it will stay alive, I decide.

Once home, I give my mother the notepad without saying a word.

I wait for Moz in the garden.

He often pads by at this time. What's keeping him?

The family secret belongs to me as well now.

I know a lot more about the who, what, where, why, how, and when.

I understand that silence can be louder than shouting.

I know that some things in your memory can carry on hurting.

I wanted to know, and now I do.

"Moz . . . ?" I whisper hopefully into the quiet garden.

No sound. Nothing.

Make sure no one can hurt you, Mama says. Don't be conspicuous, don't talk too loudly, don't make mistakes, be tidy, stay inside the lines, and always be careful everywhere you go, even if the danger is past. Be invisible, in other words.

But I'm not invisible, even if I wanted to be. I take up space, even though I'm small. And one day I won't be able to fit between the railings of the staircase anymore.

I look for Moz in the shadows of the densely planted garden. For a second, I think I see him. But I don't.

He's not coming.

I turn around and slink back inside. Almost as silently as a cat.

Hesje Jas-Querido, born 15 May 1938,
died 11 June 1943, Sobibor.

AFTERWORD

As a child, I heard about what happened to Hesje. It made a lasting impression on me. Ever since, she's always stayed in my thoughts.

Everything in this book really happened, although here and there, I've adapted the facts in order to be able to tell a well-rounded story. Most of the characters have fictional names, apart from me, my mother, her family, and of course Hesje.

Not long ago, a home movie, likely from the fall of 1939, suddenly came to light in the archive of the United States Holocaust Memorial Museum, provided by Elisheva Cohen-Paraira. Hesje can be seen in it. She walks, laughs, runs, and beams. Innocent moments, unexpectedly preserved.

A few months later, she was transported to Sobibor and gassed.

The film is old and a bit damaged; black spots flicker like dark flowers over the recording.

To view the film, visit the website of the United States Holocaust Memorial Museum: https://collections.ushmm .org/search/catalog/irn1004649 or search "Toddler at play before the war" at collections.ushmm.org.

SOME NOTES ON THIS BOOK'S PRODUCTION

The art for the jacket was created by David Wiesner,
in collaboration with Claire Williams Martinez and
Charlotte Strick of Strick&Williams, who created the concept.
David painted the artwork with Winsor & Newton
watercolors on Arches 140 lb cold press paper. For reference
he cut out paper maple leaves and a Star of David in order
to see how they could twist and bend to envelop the type.
The title and author name are set in Venti CF Bold,
a geometric font often used for headlines, logos,
and short text, designed by Connary Fagen, Inc.

The body text was set by Westchester Publishing Services
in Danbury, CT, in 11.5-point Bembo. Designed by Monotype
in 1928, Bembo is a serif typeface that was based on a design cut
by Francesco Griffo for the Venetian printer Aldus Manutius in
1495. The display text was set in Goldenbook Regular, designed
by Mark Simonson in 2003 and based on the logotype of a
literary magazine from the late 1920s called *The Golden Book
Magazine*. The book was printed on 78 gsm Yunshidai Ivory
uncoated woodfree FSC™-certified paper
and bound in China.

Production was supervised by Leslie Cohen
and Freesia Blizard
Book jacket designed by Strick&Williams
Book interiors designed by Semadar Megged
Edited by Meghan Maria McCullough

LEVINE QUERIDO